I0760783

TWISTED CROSS RANCH BOOK TWO

Corruptor's claim

K. LORAINE

USA TODAY BESTSELLING AUTHORS

MEG ANNE

Alternate Cover Edition.

ISBN:

978-1-961742-06-2 (Paperback Edition)

978-1-961742-07-9 (Hardback Edition)

Edited by Mo Sytsma of Comma Sutra Editorial

Cover Design by T.E. Black Designs

To Yellowstone, for giving us Rip Wheeler.
(That's it. That's the dedication.)

"It's the one constant in life. You build something worth having, someone's gonna try to take it."

— John Dutton, Yellowstone

corruptor's claim

K. LORAINE
USA TODAY BESTSELLING AUTHORS
MEG ANNE

authors' note

Corruptor's Claim contains mature and graphic content which may be triggering for some readers. Such content includes scenes with references to human trafficking, cuckolding, forced marriage, assault, torture, murder, and more. **Reader discretion is advised.**

As always, a detailed list of content and trigger warnings is available on our website.

one

• • •

River

There were a lot of things I hated about Twisted Cross Ranch, but the private chef's Sunday brunch spread wasn't one of them. I couldn't say the same about the man staring at me over the rim of his coffee mug, however. I'd been trying to play it cool and not let on that I was rattled by the email I'd received last night. I'd barely slept, and my nerves were shot.

"What?" I snarled at Cross as I took a fourth piece of French toast and topped it with fresh berries.

His lips quirked. "Nothing."

"If you're planning on saying anything about my meal choices, I suggest you don't."

"I didn't say anything."

"Your mouth didn't, but those judgy eyes of yours are saying a whole lot," I snapped.

He raised a brow. "Judgy eyes?"

I pointed at him and waved my finger around. "Those are judgy eyes. I'll eat what I want when I want. I know you're used to those women like *Cici* who think carbs are the devil and sugar is his bitch. That's not me. If they are, then I'm going straight to hell on a sugar rush."

His second brow lifted to join the first. "Is that so?" He balled up his napkin and tossed it on his plate. "Why don't you tell me what else you know about me? Since you seem to be the resident expert."

What the hell was happening? Usually we exchanged barbs and then I stormed off. He was . . . calm. Something was up. But he'd opened the floodgates, so I figured now was as good a time as any to get my feelings off my chest.

"You're arrogant."

"True."

"Insufferable."

"That's a matter of opinion."

I had to swallow through the wave of emotion clogging my throat before I could say what I really wanted. "The kind of asshole who takes a girl's heart and leaves it crushed at her feet the next morning without a word."

Something flashed in his eyes, but his expression and posture didn't change. "I did what I had to do."

I scoffed. "What does that even mean?" Lowering my voice, I impersonated him. *"I did what I had to do."*

"Which word precisely are you having trouble with?"

"All of it! You seemed perfectly content to take my virginity, and then you ditched me. What changed?" I wish I could say I'd maintained my tough bitch exterior, but my voice cracked a bit at the end, my vulnerability showing and pissing me off, if I was being honest. I didn't want to give him that. He'd taken too much already.

"You."

This was ridiculous. He was blaming me? "I didn't change. I was always the same stupid girl who fell in love with the boy she shouldn't want."

"You were barely eighteen, too young to know what love is."

"Don't you dare try to tell me how I felt. You were the first man I ever admitted my feelings to, and you broke something in me that night. I've built my walls so damn high no one can ever hurt me like that. Like *you*. Because of you, I've never been able to let myself fall in love again."

Wow. What was in this coffee? Truth serum? That had not been what I'd meant to say. Ever.

Eyes hard as stone, he shoved back his chair and stalked over to me. I didn't budge as he stood right in front of me, his body coiled tight, fury radiating from him. Then he reached out and took my chin, tilting my head so I was forced to meet his stare.

"I never asked you to love me, sparrow."

"And I never asked you to break my heart. But here we are."

He blew out a breath and looked away for a second, admitting softly, "If I'd have known how you felt before, I . . ."

"You what?"

His eyes returned to mine, and he shook his head. "I dunno. Maybe I'd have done things different. I wouldn't have been so careless."

"That's the perfect word to describe you, Daniel Cross Jr. Careless."

"I'm sorry. I didn't realize I was in the company of such a paragon of perfection and virtue." He stepped away, his impassive mask back in place.

Good timing, too, because Bishop chose that moment to join us, looking up from his phone in surprise when he found Cross hovering over me. Still way too close for casual conversation.

"Everything okay in here?" Bishop asked, eyeing me with concern etched on his features.

I didn't get a chance to respond because Cross's lip curled up. "Oh, look, if it isn't the man of the hour."

"What?" Bishop and I both said at the same time. I glanced over at him and smiled, mouthing, "Jinx."

Cross caught me and shook his head, muttering under his breath as he moved toward the coffeepot. "Nothing. Just clearing up some old issues between River and me. We've known each other so long it's almost impossible not to have history."

Bishop didn't take the bait, choosing to remain silent as he strode over to me. I needed to talk to him about the email I'd received. Even without the disturbing photos, it was far more threatening than the letter. I hadn't been truly afraid until now. Besides my secret agent, I didn't know who I could trust, and with Cross watching my every move, I couldn't say a word. Not until he left the room.

Bishop dropped into the empty seat next to mine and slid his calloused palm across the back of my neck. I was so surprised by the gesture that I almost missed the little squeeze he gave me before stealing one of the strawberries off my plate and popping it in his mouth.

"There's a whole ass buffet right there," I said, gesturing dramatically, although there was no hiding my smile.

Bishop simply shrugged. "It's sweeter when it's yours."

The low growl of annoyance Cross released was only echoed by his sharp, "Is that how you treated your boss the last place you worked? No wonder you came begging for a job."

Bishop laughed, startling us both. "Can't say that I did. Then again, Jake wasn't as pretty as River."

"Miss Adams," Cross snarled.

"River," I corrected, trying not to blush at Bishop calling me pretty.

The look Cross speared me with pinned me to my chair. God, he was angry. Maybe it was time to back off and let him cool down. Or maybe I could drive him away and get time alone with Bishop so he could look at that email.

And that's how Walker found us. Bishop smirking, Cross scowling, and me caught in their crosshairs, blushing and looking anywhere but at them.

"Walk—" My words dried up at the murderous expression on his face. Swallowing, I tried again. "What—"

"You're goddamn married?" he shouted.

It was so absurd I couldn't help but laugh. "What? No, I'm not."

"I'm not talking to you. Well, yeah, I kind of am." Walker turned his gaze on his brother before going right up to him and delivering a swift punch to his gut. "You married her. You've *been* married all this fucking time, and you let me fall for her. Why the fuck would you do that to me? I knew you were a dick, but I didn't think you'd stoop so low."

Cross doubled over but didn't fight back as he worked to catch his breath.

Bishop tensed beside me while I mutely shook my head. This had to be a joke. I would know if I was married.

"I'm not married. I'm pretty sure I would've had to be there."

Walker stalked over and slammed a piece of paper down on the table. "Oh, you were there."

"What?" I asked, reaching for the paper. Bishop beat me to it, his eyes quickly scanning the document before he handed it to me.

"It's legit," he murmured.

"No," I said, but I didn't sound so sure anymore. Horrified might be a more accurate description.

Cross stayed eerily silent, not meeting my gaze. This couldn't be real. It was a mistake. Or a prank. Either way, Walker was wrong. But as I stared down at my signature on the marriage certificate in my hands, I realized the only joke was on me. Because I remembered signing this document. My father had slid it over to me the night of my eighteenth birthday, assuring me it wasn't important.

"What is this again?" I'd asked my dad.

"Just some financial documents. Nothing to worry about. Your mama and I just want to make sure you're looked after if anything happens."

I trusted him, so I hadn't even checked. I just signed my whole fucking life away. A hysterical giggle escaped me as I traced the ink with a fingertip. I'd handed myself to Cross that night in more ways than one. Jesus, I hadn't just given him my virginity; we'd consummated our fucking marriage. I just hadn't known it.

"Look at me," I said, standing and squaring off with my . . . husband.

He met my stare, uncertainty in his eyes, something I wasn't used to from him.

"Did you know?"

He shook his head once, slowly. Deliberately. It was so unlike him, this lack of reaction. I wasn't sure if it was shock or guilt or some other emotion entirely. "I swear to you, River, I didn't know."

"You two expect me to believe neither one of you knew you were married? You were both stupid enough to sign a marriage certificate without reading it?" Walker ran a hand through his hair as he paced back and forth.

"I trusted my dad. It was the night of my party, the night before . . ." I trailed off, knowing they'd know which night I meant.

"He told me they were financial documents. He said this was to make sure I was taken care of. I was just a kid."

"You were old enough to get fucking married!"

"Walker, that's enough. Leave her alone." Cross coming to my defense was new. It shocked me in a way I hadn't expected.

"So what's your excuse? How did the Mighty Cross get roped into marriage?" Walker demanded, pouring himself a cup of coffee, scowling at it like it offended him, and promptly dumping the whole thing out. He was a man in crisis, but right now I was in crisis too, and I couldn't do anything to help him.

"Senior told me he needed me to sign some business papers. He was always putting shit in my name back then. I didn't even think twice."

"Idiot," Walker spat before storming to the wet bar and pulling the top off a handle of whiskey. He drank straight from the bottle, his free hand clenched in a fist.

"Walker, stop." I approached him, placing one palm on his forearm, trying to get him to look at me. "This doesn't change anything between us."

He slammed the bottle down so hard I worried it would break, then looked at me. "Yeah, it fucking does. You're my brother's wife, which means you'll never be mine." Shaking his head, he shrugged away from my touch.

Bishop had remained quiet until now. "Can't you just annul it or something? I'm not an expert on Texas law, but I'm pretty sure lack of consummation is grounds for it. Hell, you two haven't even resided in the same state in the last ten years. It's a pretty straightforward case." Cross and I must have been wearing guilty expressions because Bishop hummed and muttered, "Or not."

"That's just fucking perfect. You proud of yourself, brother? You just can't help but ruin every good thing in my life, can you?" Walker's voice was venomous as he walked away. He stopped when he reached the entrance to the kitchen, then turned pained blue eyes on me. "Welcome to the family, Mrs. Cross. I hope he's everything you ever wanted."

two

. . .

Cross

Ten years earlier

Fucking parties. It seemed like every other week we were throwing a damn party these days. Galas, weddings, engagements, and now River Adams's eighteenth birthday party. Everywhere I looked, some stranger was arranging white tulips or adjusting the candles all over the damn place. River might be my little brother's best friend, and her dad might work with us, but you'd think she was Senior's own daughter the way he was spending money on her.

"Junior, I need a minute."

My head snapped to my dad, who was standing in the mouth of the hallway leading to his office. He was dressed in his typical attire: dark jeans, black boots, a button down and blazer. The shiny belt buckle he wore was on full display, a not-so-subtle reminder he was a genuine cowboy with a rodeo history. He always poked fun at the rich boys who wore the cowboy costume but had never truly earned their spurs. It was one of the reasons Walker and I were such good riders. We'd heard his warning of, 'No son of mine will ever get away with being all hat and no cattle' more times than either of us could count.

"Now?" I asked, glancing at the circus taking place around me as if he might have forgotten we were hosting the damn thing. A whole damn band was set up in what used to be our formal living room.

"The guests should be arriving soon, so we need to get this paperwork handled before Tyson and his son get here."

"You invited our lawyers to a birthday party?" I asked as I followed him into his office.

"Good excuse as any to take care of some business."

I raised a brow. I didn't see the logic, but then my dad didn't have many friends. He had *associates*. In fact, he'd taught us early on that your inner circle should be so small you'd never have to worry about being stabbed in the back. I'd thought he was paranoid, but since he brought me in on the family business, I was starting to better understand his thought process. In our line of work, friends could easily become enemies.

Come to think of it, I wasn't sure if he'd count anyone other than Casey as an actual friend. But I knew Casey's hands were just as dirty as my dad's, and as far as Senior was concerned, Casey Adams was blood. Huh, I guess that explained the circus.

"I need you to sign a few things so we can button up some deals."

"What deals?"

"Son, there are always deals being made in our world. You're an integral part of this business now, and mergers like these are important for you to be attached to. I'll be able to rest easy knowing you're ready to take the reins once I'm gone."

"You're not going anywhere. Besides, you and I both know Casey will be there to take over if I'm not ready."

An unreadable expression crossed his face, and he made a noncommittal sound. "Be that as it may. Never hurts to be prepared."

He shoved a stack of papers at me and handed me a pen. "They're all marked for you. I already had McCreedy look them over. All you have to do is sign."

There was no arguing with him. I'd tried, and it was useless. So I sat down at the desk and began signing my life away. When I finished, he handed me a whiskey and grinned before raising it in a toast.

"Congratulations."

"For what? Knowing my name?"

He chuckled. "Something like that."

I knocked back the whiskey, relishing its burn and knowing I'd need several more to get through the night. Cecilia Davenport and her flock of gold-digging bimbos were on the prowl. I missed the days when I could fall into bed with a girl without worrying that she was going to try to trick me into more. It was a well-known truth that a single beauty queen without a diamond on her finger was on the hunt for a rich husband. I was in line to become one of the richest ranchers in the state. Scratch that. In the country.

Casey Adams walked through the door as I was refilling my glass, his green eyes flashing with amusement as he came into the room.

"All set, D?" he asked my dad.

"Yep. Signed and ready for you to look over."

"Excellent." Instead of heading to my dad, he came to me, resting his hand on my shoulder and giving me an uncharacteristically serious look. "Proud of you, son. I know you're going to take real good care of her."

"Her?"

He cleared his throat. "The business."

"It's not a ship."

My dad chuckled. "Sure it is. And you're gonna keep her afloat. Now, River's waiting for you to wish her a happy birthday. I hope you've got something nice to give her."

Why the hell was he pushing me out the door and sending me off to see his best friend's daughter, who I made it a point to barely acknowledge? I did that for a fucking reason. She'd been a gangly kid when we were growing up, easy to ignore and be annoyed by, but over the last year, River Adams had turned into a woman. A beautiful one at that. I couldn't let myself look at her now. Not without my thoughts going somewhere they shouldn't.

As of today, my reason for staying away was no longer valid, and I didn't need to flirt with temptation.

"I hadn't planned on giving her a gift. She's using my house for her party. That should be plenty."

"You know she's always been sweet on you, son."

She has?

"You sure you aren't getting me and Walker confused?"

"I know my boys. Go wish our guest of honor a happy birthday and show her a good time. She's family."

"I'm not a damn babysitter," I grumbled.

"She's not a baby," her dad pointed out.

Realizing I wasn't getting out of this, I groaned and set my glass down and grabbed the entire bottle of whiskey.

Seemed like I was going to need it.

By the time I got out to the already bustling party, my sparrow was the focus of everyone's attention. She looked so fucking pretty in her white dress, her hair falling past her shoulders, lips a cherry red as they wrapped around the straw in her drink. Damn, when had she gotten so beautiful? She wasn't like Cici or the other girls I'd grown up with. River was real and a natural beauty, just like her mama, while Cici and her crew were caked in makeup and padded bras. Those women were keeping Devil's Grove's aestheticians in business.

Walker was sitting next to her, his smile genuinely happy as they laughed together about something. She didn't need me to make her happy. Hell, I wouldn't be able to, not without breaking my self-imposed rules where she was concerned.

Instead of heading their way, I spotted Jackson and turned toward him. If I took off now, my dad would realize I was missing. At least this way, it would appear I was socializing, and Jackson was always carrying. For a lawyer's son who'd just joined his daddy's practice, the man smoked more than his share of weed. That was exactly what I needed. Oblivion and distance from the image of River's red lips wrapped around something other than her straw.

Jesus Christ. I needed to get out of here.

"McCreedy, it's been awhile . . ."

Later that night

GODDAMMIT, *Cross. Pretty sure Senior didn't mean to dick his partner's daughter down when he told you to show her a good time.*

I was supposed to stay away. How was sticking my dick in her staying away? The answer? It wasn't. But fuck, she was everything. River stared at me like I was her whole world as I made love to her, and if I was being honest, in that moment, she was mine. I wanted to take care of her and make sure she felt protected and cherished. The second my sparrow kissed me in that gazebo, I was done for.

I should feel bad about taking her virginity, but I couldn't muster an ounce of guilt. Not when I knew for a fact any other man she gave herself to would have treated her like her pleasure didn't matter. I took my time and focused on her, made her come until she was near tears. I made it good for her. Special.

But I also couldn't lie to myself and say this meant nothing to me. This wasn't a one-time thing between us. Not with the way my heart was racing or how she was looking at me. Not to mention who she was. If Casey found out what I just did to his baby girl, I wouldn't be surprised to find myself on the business end of a shotgun being marched down the aisle.

He's the one who said she wasn't a baby . . .

So not a fucking excuse, man. You are so screwed.

And then she looked up at me with those big eyes while I was still pulsing inside her and whispered three words that solidified everything I'd been thinking.

"I love you."

I froze, the magnitude of that admission hitting me like a ton of bricks. Plenty of girls had said it to me, hoping I'd be their forever. None of them made me feel like River did. The trouble with her was, I could actually see it. The future with her in my arms.

Something shifted in me, determination and purpose aligning. I'd gone about this all wrong, but that changed right fucking now. Instead of responding with empty words, I dropped a kiss on her forehead and pulled out of her. "I'll be right back, sparrow."

Her eyelids were already drooping as she hummed a soft, happy sound. Then I got up on shaky legs, disposing of the condom and bringing a blanket over to cover her before I slipped in beside her. She sighed in her sleep, and I buried my face in her sweet-smelling hair, just letting myself be happy for once. That one thought crystallized in my mind. *She* made me happy.

Just one night laughing and flirting with her, and I was a goner. My mama had told me about magic like that. How when you found your person it was like the stars aligned and you just knew. It's what she had with my dad. Why they'd married so young after only dating a few weeks.

When you know, you know.

I fucking knew.

There was no way I'd ignore this feeling. She said she loved me, gave it to me without me asking, but I had some work to do to earn it. When she woke up, I'd start over with her. She deserved so much more than my bullshit, grumpy asshole act. I'd take my time and court her properly, ask her daddy's permission to make her mine, throw my hat in the ring so everyone knew she belonged with me.

Now that I'd decided on a path, I was ready to make it happen. But she was young; she deserved a chance to do all the things a girl her age would want to do. It'd be hard, but I could be patient, knowing she was my prize in the end. By the time I was done, I'd prove to the both of us that I was worthy of her love.

My phone started buzzing where it had fallen on the floor. I looked over at it with a curse, not wanting to move away from the woman snuggled up next to me. When the buzzing stopped only to immediately start up again, I knew it had to be Senior.

Fuck, I couldn't ignore this.

THREE HOURS LATER, I stood over River's sleeping form covered in blood and stained with the night's sins. Three hours. That's all it had taken for my plans of a happily ever after to go up in flames.

I couldn't keep her. I couldn't let her anywhere near the horror show that was my life.

It would destroy her, and I couldn't be the reason for her destruction.

So I'd let her go. Doing so would destroy *me*, but I'd rather be the one to suffer so she could stay free and happy.

With shaking hands, I scrawled a note I knew would shatter her heart and make her hate me, but it was for the best. I'd rather hurt her now, knowing she'd be alive. Safe. Untouched by this madness.

The last thing she needed was ties to this family. So I had to make sure she never had a reason to come back to me. Because life with me wouldn't just be a cage, it would be a noose, slowly suffocating everything good and pure inside her. I couldn't be the reason the light left her eyes. I had to let my sparrow fly free.

It felt like my fucking soul protested each brush of pen on paper, but I forced myself to keep going. To make a clean break. My stomach churned as I finished the worst letter I'd ever written and laid it next to her so she'd be sure to see it along with the box of Plan B I'd picked up on my way home as soon as she opened her eyes.

RIVER,

THANKS FOR THE RIDE. I SHOULD'VE BEEN CLEAR LAST NIGHT.

THIS WAS A ONE-TIME DEAL. I DON'T WANT TO BE TIED DOWN TO SOME KID WHO DOESN'T KNOW HOW TO HANDLE ME.

TAKE THE PILL WHEN YOU WAKE UP. THE LAST THING WE NEED IS ANOTHER MISTAKE.

C

I stared down at her and had to fight the urge to brush a lock of hair away from her pretty face. This was for the best. It had to be this way.

Cross, you motherfucker, you're going to burn in hell for this.

But as I turned and walked away, I knew the truth.

I was already there.

three

. . .

Cross

Walker continued spouting off his jealous bullshit. Let's call a spade a spade; his tantrum was one hundred percent fueled by jealousy.

"You done?" I asked when he paused at the entryway.

"So fucking done," he muttered.

"About damn time," I said, snatching the document off the table and making my own hasty retreat.

"Where are you going?" River shot her question at me with all the force of a bullet.

I couldn't even look at her right now. My mind was too full of the emotional shrapnel from that grenade Walker just lobbed at us. But was it a grenade if it had been sitting there unnoticed for a decade? This was more like a landmine.

"To call my fucking lawyer."

"Shouldn't I—"

"Let him cool off, siren," Bishop murmured, interrupting whatever River had been about to say and snagging her hand as she attempted to follow me.

"Get your hands off my wife," I snarled.

Fuck, where had that come from?

I kept my eyes locked on the place where Bishop touched her, fury spiking when neither of them made any attempt to move. By any measuring stick, it was innocent, but the protectiveness behind the gesture needled me. Did he really think I'd hurt her?

River's voice snapped me back to the present.

"I'm not your wife."

"This paperwork says different."

"How convenient. I'm sure you're pleased as punch to know you've got me even more chained to you now."

I let out a huff but couldn't deny the twinge of possessive energy the title of husband sent through me. Legally, she was mine, but it didn't make a damn bit of difference, not now that I'd made her hate me. And maybe fear me. Dammit. That was the part that was really bothering me. We hadn't spoken, not really, since the night with the Russian. I had no fucking idea what was going through her head when she looked at me. But it didn't take a rocket scientist to tell it wasn't remotely friendly, let alone *wifely*.

"I'll take care of it."

"Will you? I want a divorce, Cross."

That word hit me with the force of a freight train. I'd always said when I married it would be for keeps—of course, that was before I realized marriage was never in the cards for me. It's how I'd managed to stay a bachelor into my late twenties. Then the night I spent with River changed everything. I'd had to give her up, and when I did that, I knew my one chance at forever was gone. No one would ever measure up. No one would make me feel the way she had. And even if they had, they'd be in the line of fire just like she would have been. So why try?

The devil on my shoulder started crooning in my ear, and fuck me if he wasn't speaking a world of sense.

But she's already in their crosshairs now. Divorcing her won't change that. She'll always be tied to you, which means they'll always be able to use her against you. So you might as well keep her. It's what you always wanted. You ruined her life without having to do a damn thing. Might as well enjoy the flames while you burn together.

"No."

"Excuse me?"

"You heard me. You want some easy uncontested divorce? You're not getting it."

Her eyes flashed with green fire, and I could tell she immediately jumped to the conclusion that painted me in the worst light. "You just want my shares. Figures the thing that blows up my entire life is the same thing that brings you joy. I bet you see this as your saving grace."

"So what if I do?"

Only River could be so fucking wrong and so completely right all at the same time. I hadn't even considered the shares, to be honest. I'd been too wrapped up in the part where she'd been mine for the last ten years and neither of us knew about it. But now that she'd mentioned it, it was a good cover. Keeping the shares would give me the excuse I needed to contest the divorce while I tried to win her back. I'd had her heart once; I could have it again.

Probably.

Okay, maybe not. But I had to try. I wasn't going to let her go again without a fight. It nearly killed me the last time.

She huffed and shook her head. "I'm getting my divorce, Cross."

"The hell you are."

"We'll see about that," she grumbled, standing up and walking to the window, keeping her back to me. This time Bishop let her go, but he continued to watch us with the intensity of a hawk waiting to strike.

I almost went to her but held myself back. She was madder than a nest of hornets, and while fighting with her made me want her even more, I had a call to make.

My phone was to my ear as soon as I left the kitchen, McCreedy answering on the first ring. I didn't give the man time to so much as speak.

"Why the fuck was I not your first call?"

"I'm sorry, Cross. Walker asked me to get everything in order so he and River could get hitched. I . . . Hell, I thought you must've known."

I scoffed, striding into my suite and slamming the door behind me. It was too early in the day for a drink, but I really fucking needed one. "You thought I knew? You thought I'd go to the lengths I've gone to keep this place after she was given most of our goddamned legacy while knowing I'm already entitled to half of everything she owns?"

"It's your signature on the certificate. I know your serial killer scrawl better than my own handwriting."

"She wants a divorce."

"I've already started drawing up the papers."

"Throw them away."

"What?"

"I want to keep her."

He was silent for a beat, letting my admission hang there like a pendulum suspended in time. "Your brother wants to marry her."

"Well, that's too damn bad, now isn't it?"

I could practically feel the wheels spinning in my attorney's head. "You don't even like the woman, Cross."

"My feelings for her aren't any of your business. I only need you to handle the paperwork."

The soft sound of a pen tapping on paper filled the line before he asked, "This about that Russian?"

He thought I was falling back on Walker's excuse, marrying her to keep her the hell away from Dominik. I could work with that. It was damn near the truth anyway.

"Sure."

"And when she files for herself?"

"Bury her in legal red tape. Buy me as much time as you can. She'll come around."

Probably. There was no escaping that knowing little voice in my head as it parroted my earlier thoughts.

"I guess she's safer married to one of you. But she might kill you herself at this rate."

"I'll take the risk."

He sighed. "And Walker? What about him?"

"He'll get over it."

"Doubtful."

Too damn bad.

"He doesn't have a fucking choice."

River was mine. She had been for ten years. Now I just had to dig my heels in and do the work to make her want to stay that way.

I just wasn't sure how I'd get her to change her mind about me after everything I'd done to push her away. But that was future me's problem. Dominik had his sights set on my wife, and if he was going to be deterred, he had to know she wouldn't be lured away from me. That couldn't happen if she visibly hated me. Unfortunately, it would take time to repair the damage I'd caused, and that was the one thing I didn't have. Yet.

Money couldn't buy me love, but it sure as hell could buy me time.

"Send a press release announcing our marriage. Every fucking person in the state of Texas needs to know she's mine. Especially Dominik Volkov."

Desperate times called for desperate measures never rang so true.

"That's not really my job, Cross."

"It is now. I pay you obscene amounts of money, Jackson. You'll do whatever the fuck I tell you to do."

We'd had enough of these conversations over the years that I knew the vein in his temple would be pulsing while he mentally called me every vile name in the book. But all he said was, "I'll take care of it."

"See that you do."

"Anything else?"

I didn't give myself time to second-guess my impulse. If I was going to war with Volkov, I may not survive it. "Set up a trust for her. If anything happens to me, I want to know she'll be taken care of."

"She's your wife—"

"The money is hers, even if the divorce goes through."

McCreedy blew out a heavy breath. "Oh, hell. You don't hate her. You're fucking in love with her."

I hung up on him.

four

. . .

River

Walker and Bishop were silent sentinels in the kitchen as I stared blankly out the window. Now that Cross had made his grand exit, neither seemed to have a reason to leave, and I could feel both men taking up space in the room. I knew I had to talk to them each on their own, try to make them understand how I felt about this situation, but the truth was, I hadn't even processed it myself yet.

Ten years ago, I would've married the hell out of Cross. I would've fallen into his arms and ridden off into the sunset with him, no questions asked. Now? The reality of us was so different. He was nothing like the man I'd thought he was.

But you're not that same girl either.

There was no way we could stay married. Right?

I mean hell, I'd just fucked his brother. Was it fucking when it was that slow and drawn out? And then there was what happened with Sterling against the wall of the club. Jesus, I was still getting flutters thinking about it.

So much for my dry spell. When it rains, it fucking pours. I went from single with no prospects to married with two mistresses. Could a man be a mistress? A Mister-ess?

I blew out a frustrated breath, my thoughts not helping matters at all.

Bishop's large frame pressed against my back, his fingers slipping across my nape as he leaned close. "I'll give you time with him if you need it. But you and I are having our own discussion about what this means later, siren. And I'm not going far. Call me if you need me."

His touch sent shivers down my spine. That was the third time this morning he'd touched me. I'd cataloged each and every press of his fingers against my skin. Something had changed between us last night, and he now felt comfortable enough to initiate touch regularly. I mean, his fingers had been inside me, so perhaps that was an obvious statement. But knowing what I did of his past, I couldn't dismiss the significance. Nor did I want to. It mattered to me that he felt safe enough to let his guard down this much. I didn't want to lose that because of a stupid piece of paper I knew nothing about.

I glanced over my shoulder at Walker, who was leaning against the counter, arms crossed, expression wounded. He'd stopped looking at me and was intently inspecting the tile floor instead.

"I'm okay. I'll come find you later, and I promise, if I need you, I'll call."

His silver eyes bore into mine for several heartbeats before he nodded. Part of me thought he might kiss me, ached for it even, but he just gave my neck a gentle squeeze before he left Walker and me alone.

Walker made a disgusted sound. "You really think you're going to need to call him? Because of me?"

"There's more than one way to hurt someone, Walker. Not all scars are visible."

He flinched, knowing exactly what I was alluding to. His gifts last night had been sweet and terribly thoughtful, but it didn't automatically undo the hurt he and Cross had caused.

"I'm trying to prove to you I'm worth your attention, ladybug. I'd lay down my life for you if you asked me to. Knowing you had reason not to trust me, not to love me back, was painful, but I had a plan. I was confident I could win you back and earn your trust again. But then this? You're married to Cross. I . . ." He shook his head, hands fisting.

"Where does that even leave me? Say you two get divorced. There's still no way I can slide in after that. I'd always be second choice."

"Walker, marrying him was never a choice. Not one I made, anyway."

His eyes burned as they met mine. "But you never chose me either. Not really."

"I'm choosing myself right now. It's the only option that keeps me safe."

He pushed off the counter and took a couple steps toward me. "I can keep you safe, darlin'. I *want* to."

God, I wished I could give in and just let him do that for me. But there was too much at stake. I was caught in Cross's web, and the only way to get out was to cut myself free.

"Isn't the saying the road to hell is paved with good intentions?"

"I guess that's the difference between you and me. I'd go to hell every single time if it's where you were. Beside you is the only place I want to be."

Damn him and his sweet words. I could feel my resolve slipping with every step closer. I'd cave if he touched me. Did I want to cave? Was I just being stubborn?

"Walker, you can't say things like that to me."

"Why not? It's true. Saying anything less than that would be a bald-faced lie, and I promised you we'd only have truth between us."

I bit down on my lip, shaking my head at him, because I had no idea what to say. What *could* I say?

"I kissed Bishop," I blurted.

Well, that's one option, you freaking idiot.

"You already told me about that."

"Again, I mean. Last night."

He prowled closer, this time close enough to reach over and tip my chin up. "Just a kiss?"

I shook my head, heart racing. "No."

"Did you let him touch you?"

"Yes."

"Where?"

Did he mean where on my body, or . . .? I went with option B. "Outside at the gala."

His lips twitched. "Did he make you come?"

I nodded, not trusting my voice.

"Sneaky bastard."

I was surprised he seemed to be taking this so well after the way he'd come in hot under the collar this morning.

"I already know I'm not the only man in your heart. It's never just been me. But now I know I'll have to make sure I keep you thinking of me even when you've got him in your bed."

"K-keep me? B-both of you?" I stuttered, thoughts of Walker and Sterling sandwiching me between them suddenly taking over my mind and rendering me stupid. This conversation was not going in the direction I thought it would.

His brows rose, and a mischievous glint shone in his eyes. "Is that something you'd want? You riding me while he's got his hands on you? Or me fucking you from behind while his dick is in your hot little mouth?"

I think I had a stroke. My mind emptied, and I was utterly speechless. "Jesus, Walker," I finally breathed, my panties absolutely destroyed by those mental images. I was going to need a long shower after this.

He leaned in and feathered his lips over my pulse point, his scruff tickling my neck. "You wouldn't have to choose between us. We could both make you feel so good, darlin'. If my cock made you cry, the two of us together would make you weep."

A little gasp was all I was capable of as I rolled the thought around in my mind. The more I thought about it, the more attractive it was. But how would that work? Surely one or both of them would want me to choose eventually. And who's to say Sterling would ever be okay with something like this? It would never work. It was a fool's dream. A fucking hot one, but a dream.

And then there was the little matter of my secret husband.

"What would Cross have to say about that?"

Walker stiffened. Only a little, but I noticed. "You asked for a divorce, so what does it matter? Besides, we're already having an illicit affair. You were married to him when I made love to you in the cabin. Remember how good we were together? White hot, passionate, perfect."

"You say that like I knew, but I didn't. I never would have . . ." I loosed a heavy sigh. This was a pointless conversation. "I'm not a cheater, Walker."

"I know. And what you're doing with Bishop and me ain't cheating either. We know about each other. Cross knows about us. I'm just suggesting we make this a team sport if that would make you feel better about it."

"Cross won't share."

"Cross doesn't deserve you, and a piece of paper you were tricked into signing means nothing."

He made an excellent point. Still, my brows furrowed. "You're sure singing a different tune than when you stormed in here. You were hell-bent on crucifying the both of us."

"That's when I thought you'd been keeping me in the dark. Now that I know there's still hope . . ." He shrugged, as if it were obvious.

The way he said that made my heart ache. If things were different, we might have a shot at a future, but everything had changed with my marriage to his brother. I could never resign myself to a life where I was constantly lying to the man I was married to. Marriage, to me, meant partnership. Trust. Fidelity. I wanted what my parents had. I wanted love. Anything less would be settling, and I refused to do that. Not even for Walker.

Not that I'm staying married to Cross.

No way.

"I love you, River. I'll take you whatever way I can have you. Just tell me it's not too late. Just a glimmer of hope. That's all I need."

He closed the distance between us, brushing his lips over mine, but I backed away. I couldn't be with him. "There isn't any. We can't do this. As soon as my divorce is final, I'm leaving. It's over."

Walker's hurt washed over me, his words cold and biting. "Looks like you're making a choice after all."

I had to get out of here, away from the man whose heart I had to break because it was killing me to see him like this. Shoving out of his hold, I made a beeline for the back door, desperate to trade the anguish of this moment for the suffocating heat of a Texas afternoon.

"You're right, I am. Like I already told you, I'm choosing me."

five

. . .

Bishop

The steady clank of the weights was my only companion as I tried to work through my frustration. It had been three hours since I left River alone to talk to Walker. After the first, I'd decided to come down to the gym and blow off some steam. What was taking them so long? Did she need me? Had he won her over and convinced her to fall back into bed with him?

Stop it, Bishop. You're not doing yourself any favors following that line of thought.

But even though I knew better, I couldn't help myself. Not even twenty-four hours ago, my fingers had been buried inside her slick cunt, her moans against my lips. It made me possessive. Hungry for more. Dammit, I couldn't get hard right now. I was trying to distract myself, not add to my misery.

I counted out the last of my reps before switching arms and starting over. Sweat trickled down my back as I counted each controlled lift. One. Two. Three . . . and I swore I could smell her perfume in the air.

"She's not yours. Let her be." I spoke the words aloud, hoping I might believe them if I heard them with my own ears. She wasn't mine.

But for a moment last night, she had been. And I wasn't ready to give her up.

We hadn't talked about it being anything more. There hadn't exactly been time, but part of me had hoped we might be on the same page about seeing where things might go. See if she'd let me tie her up and have my way with her. Give her so many orgasms she nearly passed out from the pleasure.

Focus, Bishop.

Not that I was ready for a relationship. Right? Fuck, I didn't even know what I wanted except that I wanted more of her.

Did that make me an asshole? Should I step aside and let her work out her shit with Walker and Cross? That's what a good man would do.

But I wasn't a good man.

Not anymore.

A little gasp from behind me had my muscles clenching, the hairs standing up on the back of my neck. I hadn't even noticed she was there. It was Volkov all over again. I really was getting sloppy. This woman twisted me up so much I couldn't even do the job I'd spent nearly a decade training for.

Working to keep my cool, I turned my head and found River standing in the open doorway, her eyes heated as she took in my shirtless torso.

"You three one big happy family now?" I asked, hating how jealous I sounded as I set the barbell down.

"Hardly." She didn't flinch. My siren entered the gym and approached me, her gaze not on mine but trained on my back and shoulders.

On instinct, I turned around to face her, trying to hide the overlapping scars I knew she'd seen, their thick and jagged ridges as familiar to me as the freckles on the back of my hand.

"What happened to you, Sterling? Who did that?"

I shrugged. "Lots of people."

"Is that why you don't like to be touched?"

She wasn't pulling her punches today, was she? The last thing I wanted was for her to hear about the months of torture I'd endured behind enemy lines. How close to death I'd been more than once. How

I couldn't close my eyes without seeing them looming over me for years after I'd come home. She didn't need to carry that weight.

No one did.

I knew she wanted an answer. Deserved one, even, but she already had it. The truth was in the marks that covered me. My back was the worst of it, by far. But there were burns and other scars across my torso. There was no hiding what had been done to me.

"All at once or over time?" Her question was soft as she reached out like she might touch me. It took everything in me not to shrink away, but she stopped herself, her fingers shaking as she lowered her arm to her side.

"Over time. They waited until I was healed enough not to die of shock or blood loss."

Why was I fucking telling her this? My darkness wasn't her burden to bear.

I don't know what I expected her to say, but her growled, "I hope you killed them. Slowly," was not fucking it. Maybe my siren had a little darkness of her own.

"They're dead and buried."

"Good. There's a special place in hell for people who would do something like that."

"I was wrong about you."

"What?"

"You're not a siren. You're a shark."

She flashed her teeth, then grinned. "Sirens are deadly too, Bishop."

"I told you to call me Sterling."

"You're not inside me. I thought we saved that for those occasions?"

So she wasn't choosing a Cross brother over me. I'd been hopeful when she sidestepped my question, but this flirtatious behavior proved it. Blood rushed to my dick, and I had to shift to make sure she didn't notice the way my mesh shorts tented.

"I like my name on your lips whenever you say it. But I can be inside you again if that's what you need."

My voice had dropped to the husky rasp I'd used last night. The color staining her cheeks told me she recognized it. But it was the way her pupils dilated and her pulse started to throb along the side of her neck that told me she wanted it.

She might legally share their last name, but she was still mine.

The proof was right there in front of me.

I knew if I touched her right now, she'd welcome it. That I could have her on her back screaming my name in seconds. But not before we addressed the elephant in the room.

"What happened with Walker, siren?"

"I'm not going to lie and tell you there's nothing between us."

I nodded, letting her know that it was okay, that I wasn't upset by her honesty, even if it felt a bit like she'd sucker punched me.

Her eyes darted around the gym before returning to my steady gaze. "He knows about you too. It's all so complicated, Sterling. I don't know which way is up."

"What about Cross?"

Her eyes hardened. "It's nothing."

"The hallway didn't look like nothing. The way he watches you doesn't look like nothing, either. And now it turns out you two are married. That's something."

An annoyed huff left her lips as she crossed her arms over her chest and backed away from me. "I'll be divorced before I can get used to signing my new name. He doesn't matter."

There was no mistaking her determination, but I'd been paying attention to her. Studying her tells. Memorizing every little detail. She was lying. I just wasn't sure if it was to herself or to protect me. Had she really convinced herself Cross didn't have her as tangled up as she did him?

Whatever the reason, I didn't think she'd appreciate me calling her out on it. But that wasn't the only thought crowding my mind. I always did my best thinking while working out, and I'd come to realize in the last couple hours that being Cross's wife might offer her more protection than she knew. If I'd learned anything during my time watching Cross, it was that he protected what was his.

I'd seen how Volkov looked at her last night. I knew he was making a play, and it was clear she was part of it. A messy divorce would put her out in the open, vulnerable—easy prey for a man like that.

"Why are you looking at me like that?"

"Like what?"

"Like you don't believe me."

"Oh, I believe you want a divorce. I'm just not sure it's the best idea."

"What?" Her shock couldn't have been any greater. "How the hell can you say that? Maybe if you knew what he did to me, you'd see how fucking ridiculous that is."

I was about to explain my thought process when my attention snagged on something she'd said. "What the fuck did he do to you? Did he hurt you?"

"If breaking my eighteen-year-old heart counts, yes. I thought I was in love with him ten years ago. I thought, stupidly, he was my white knight and the two of us would have a fairytale life together. Instead he took my virginity, then threw me away with nothing more than a note. I left for Alaska the next day."

Motherfucking playboy. No wonder she hated him so much. But the words she'd said echoed in my mind as well. She'd thought she was in love. You didn't just get over something like that.

"You can't get a divorce."

Her mouth fell open, a little noise of surprise escaping. "I can't?"

"No. Not yet."

Her eyes narrowed. "What aren't you telling me?"

A whole fucking lot, siren.

"Do you trust me?"

"I thought I did, but I'm questioning myself right now."

I blew out a breath. That was fair. I needed to give her something.

"That man we ran into last night."

"What about him?"

"He's a bad guy."

"Who the fuck among us . . ."

I snickered, because she had a point. She was surrounded by gunslingers and mobsters, and from the sound of it, had been raised by a motorcycle club. The girl had seen some shit.

"No. I mean *bad*, siren. The worst. And he's set his sights on you."

"What?" She laughed. "I don't even know the guy. He saw me for like ten seconds."

I shook my head. "That's all it takes."

I should fucking know.

"So what does being married have to do with him?"

"If you're *happy* with Cross, not able to be swayed, he can't touch you without starting a war."

She opened her mouth, then closed it again, eyeing me warily. My secret was out now, one of them, anyway, and she knew that meant I had access to all kinds of classified information. And she was smart enough to put together that I wasn't here working for Cross for the fun of it. She must have figured out Cross was under investigation; she just didn't know why. But I guessed she was starting to put the pieces together.

"Stay married to Cross—for now."

"Do you know what you're asking me?"

"I'm asking you to stay alive."

Her expression softened. "How long?"

"As long as it takes. Cross can protect you better than you can protect yourself."

She let out a humorless laugh. "We'll kill each other."

"You loved him once. You can tolerate him for a while." Unable to resist, I pinched her chin between my fingers and thumb, tipping her face up so she knew I was serious. "I won't let him hurt you, siren. You aren't alone."

"Promise?"

I closed the distance between us and feathered a kiss over her lips. "With my life. I won't let anything happen to you, I swear it."

"Why are you helping me? Does this have anything to do with what happened to my parents?"

That was a simple question with a complicated answer.

"I'd have helped you with that regardless. It's sort of my job to help people."

"So if not because of them or out of some sense of duty, then why?"

"Because you made me care, and I haven't cared about anything in a long fucking time."

Rising onto her toes, she presented her lips to me, waiting for me to make the move and kiss her. Even now, she respected my boundaries.

"How long has it been?" she asked.

My gaze was locked on her full lips. I couldn't deny her, not now, not ever. I brushed my mouth across hers and gave her one more soft kiss before whispering, "A long. Fucking. Time."

six

. . .

Walker

I stared down at the nearly empty pint glass in front of me as the hum of music blended with the deep murmurs of the bar patrons' conversations. I wasn't here to socialize. I was nursing my broken heart and washing away the pain with alcohol.

Yesterday had been bad enough. Finding out they'd been married all this time and River telling me to kick rocks after I poured my heart out to her. But then my asshole brother had to go and add insult to injury.

My lip curled in a snarl as the headline that had greeted me on the front page of the morning's paper scrolled across the dive bar's lone TV:

DANIEL CROSS JR. (BILLIONAIRE BACHELOR AND RANCHER ROYALTY) FINALLY MARRIES CHILDHOOD SWEETHEART IN SECRET WEDDING

I gripped the glass so hard I was surprised it didn't crack under the pressure. "Childhood sweetheart? She was *my* fucking childhood sweetheart." I knocked back the remnants of my drink, forcing myself to look away when a photo of River and Cross appeared on the screen. It had been taken the night of the gala. I remembered clearly because I should've been in the damn photo, but they'd cropped me and Bishop out for this story.

"They make a nice couple, don't they?" A highball glass filled with whiskey slid across the table to me as Tex took a seat.

"Nice isn't the word I'd use." I cocked a brow at him. "Did I say you could sit down?"

"Since when do I need an invite? We're practically family."

I scoffed. "Family hasn't done anything but make me fucking angry lately. Don't know if that's what you're going for, but you sure seem to be headed down that same path."

Tex gave me a considering look, nursing his own drink. "You need someone to take your anger out on? I know a couple places you might be able to do some damage. A little retaliation for the herd we lost a few weeks back."

That perked me up. A fight sounded like exactly what the doctor ordered, and since I couldn't go after the man responsible for ruining my life, a stand-in would do nicely.

"You found them?"

"We tracked them down this morning. A couple of the guys and I'll be heading out around midnight to pay a call and take back what's ours."

"Count me in."

Tex nodded as if he'd expected nothing less. Then he tilted his head toward the TV again. "I thought he didn't even like her. Shows what I know, huh?" he said with a little chuckle.

Any excitement I had about the night fizzled out as my reason for being here came crashing back down on me. I knocked back the nearly full glass of whiskey, relishing the burn.

"I don't know what he's thinking, but she matters to us both. I just really thought it'd be me."

Tex whistled. "That's some real soap opera shit right there."

"What do you know about soap operas?"

"My gran used to make me watch that hospital one with her."

"Uh huh."

He grunted and rolled his eyes. "I like Yellowstone, okay? That Rip guy isn't half bad."

"Found yourself a role model, didja?" I eyed his dusty hat and vest. I could see it.

"Maybe I did." He grinned. "It gets my boots under plenty of beds. Especially once I grew the beard."

I simply shook my head, unable to come up with a retort for that one. "Call me when y'all are ready, and I'll meet you."

"Will do, boss. And in the meantime, if you need me, you know where to reach me." Tex stood and gestured for the waitress as he tipped his hat to me.

I groaned inwardly as the pretty brunette sashayed toward me, deep brown eyes sparkling with flirtatious energy I knew well. "What can I do for you, sugar?"

"Hey, Tina. Looking good, as always."

"Not good enough to get you to take me out again, apparently."

Tina and I had dated in high school, then shared an on-again-off-again situation over a few years. We'd had an understanding. Any time we were both single, we'd help scratch that itch. Friends with benefits, except we weren't friends.

"I'm not single."

"You look plenty single to me."

"Looks can be deceiving."

She pouted. "And here I thought you showing up tonight was a sign."

"A sign I need a damn drink. How long have you worked here?"

"Couple of months. Anton got me a job here. He likes to watch me work."

She rested her hip against my table, making the scraps of fabric she called clothes ride up higher. The girl was showing so much skin, she wouldn't be out of place at a topless bar. I could see why her man wanted to keep an eye on her. Especially if she made a habit out of getting friendly with her customers.

"Wait, if you're dating someone . . ."

She winked. "I've always got room in my schedule for you, Walker Cross. Now, if you're not gonna take me home tonight, what can I get you?"

"Another one of these." I lifted my pint glass, opting for more beer rather than whiskey since I planned on *working* later. "And keep 'em coming."

"You got it, handsome."

HOURS LATER, I'd finally settled my tab and pulled myself up by my bootstraps. I wasn't gonna let River go easily, not when I knew for a fact she still wanted me, but I'd come to a decision. I'd give her some space, keep her in my line of sight and make sure she was protected, but I was still firmly keeping myself out of the friend zone. She might be my brother's wife, but she was my everything.

Until I could have her again, I'd throw myself into the family business, the *real* business. Cross had been following our trucks and trying to figure out who our rat was. I could take that over. I could be just as convincing as he was. Lord knows I wouldn't have any trouble beating the shit out of someone until they wanted to talk. And I certainly had a little extra anger to purge these days. I didn't see that changing anytime soon. Not until River changed her mind.

Palming my keys, I stepped out of the bar and into the warm humid night, annoyed as all get out that all but one of the lights in the parking lot had burned out. Fucking dive bars. Once you left, they didn't care if you fell on your face and died, as long as it didn't happen under their roofs.

I only made it a few steps before I dropped my keys, swaying slightly. I had to brace myself on the useless lamppost in order to keep from falling as I scooped my keys off the pavement. It took four tries.

Fuck.

I was drunker than I thought. No way I could drive home like this. Time to find a ride. Maybe Tina would oblige. She liked me. She wouldn't stomp all over my heart and marry my brother.

Actually, I was pretty sure she would jump at the chance to be his. Every-fucking-one would. That motherfucker—

I didn't get a chance to finish my tirade before something hard flew into my face and sent me spinning. Instant agony ripped across my cheek, and my vision went black for a moment as I worked to keep my balance.

"The fuck?"

"Damn, I thought he was actually going to put up a fight." My attacker's amused laughter would've had me kicking his ass if I wasn't so damn drunk.

"Give him a second. Not like you gave him a chance," a second, gravelly voice replied.

"You critiquing me?"

"Just sayin'. They call it a sucker punch for a reason."

The two voices floated above me as I blinked to clear my eyes. I didn't recognize either of them, but this didn't feel like a random attack.

"Well, let's make sure he sees the rest of these coming," the shit-talker said.

I tried to dodge as his fist came toward my face, but there was too much alcohol in my system, and my reactions were slower than normal. Brass knuckles slammed into my chin, splitting my lip. Great. My face was gonna be ruined. River liked my face.

I was doubled over, still not seeing clearly. Like an idiot, I'd left my gun at home. Cross would never let me live it down—unless these guys killed me, of course. And I'd dropped my keys again during that first blow to the head, so the only weapons I had on me were my fists and my brain. And I think my brain was taking a lunch. Concussions tended to do that to you, and with the way the lights were going all squiggly, I had a hunch I might have one.

Not sure what the fuck else to do, I ran toward the guy closest to me, hoping to tackle him so I could start throwing some punches of my own. I might be outnumbered, but I wasn't going down without a fight.

They were ready for me, though, and within moments I was on my back on the dirty ground, trying and failing to get away from their well-placed and vicious kicks. I saw stars when one of them got me in the side, right where I'd been stabbed a few weeks back. The pain was unbearable, causing me to roll over and bring up everything I'd had to drink that night.

Fuck, they really were trying to kill me. And I couldn't even find the breath to ask what I'd done to deserve it. Maybe I'd fucked one of their girlfriends. That sounded like me.

"That's enough," a deep accented voice said, thankfully making them stop their assault on my sides. "I'll take it from here."

"Fucking . . . Russian . . . cocksucker," I wheezed.

The man above me tsked. I could just barely make out the lines of his suit and the black metal bar he held loosely in his hand.

"Now, is that any way to speak to a friend?"

Friend? Motherfucker, you're trying to kill me.

None of that came out, though. I just groaned and spat out a mouthful of blood.

"I hope you weren't planning on running any marathons, Mr. Cross," the Russian said, kneeling beside me and speaking conversationally, like he wasn't threatening me with a crowbar.

"Why?"

"Because you won't be able to walk when I'm through with you." He patted me on the leg like it was no big deal before he stood and shifted his weight. The change in position allowed the glimmer of light from the one fucking lamp to reflect in his eyes. Raising the weapon, he brought it down on my leg so hard the bone audibly snapped.

I couldn't help it. A scream tore from my throat.

"Oh, and Mr. Cross, please do tell your brother that Dominik sends his regards."

Then he slammed the crowbar down once more for good measure, and I succumbed to the pain as the world went black.

seven

• • •

River

My phone dinged on the desk, pulling me from the spreadsheet analysis I'd been trying and failing to complete. To say I was distracted was a complete understatement. Ever since yesterday's surprise announcement, I couldn't focus on a damn thing, and it was all Cross's fault. As usual.

GIGI:

Excuse me, what the fuck is this?

The screen lit up with a link to the latest news article announcing my joyous union with Daniel Cross Jr., and I groaned in pure frustration.

ME:

Don't believe everything you read. Also, it's fucking early. Why are you awake?

GIGI:

I could ask you the same question. Don't try to distract me from my question. Are you married to the cowboy equivalent of Bruce Wayne?

I snorted at the mental image. Cross was so far from a hero, vigilante or otherwise.

ME:

He's more like . . .

I ended up deleting my text because I couldn't think of a better comparison.

GIGI:

I see those bouncing dots. Stop overthinking. Just answer the question, are you or are you not a married woman?

ME:

Are.

ME:

Apparently I have been for ten years.

GIGI:

Now it was Gigi's turn for bouncing dots. They went on and on, never delivering a message. Great, I'd broken her.

ME:

Hello? Was that it? The moment you finally realized I wasn't worth all the shit that came with being my friend?

GIGI:

Ten years? How have you been his wife for ten years without knowing it?

How did I answer this delicately? There was a lot more to this than I could divulge.

ME:

Let's just say the paperwork was buried. Deep.

GIGI:

And how did you find out?

ME:

Walker.

Come to think of it, how did Walker get his hands on the information? I didn't think to ask in the middle of everything else.

GIGI:

Well, this is a development.

ME:

I think of it more as a fucking nightmare, you know, since I'm in the middle of it.

GIGI:

Oh my God, you're like . . . living a romance novel trope. Secret marriage. Broody billionaire. Enemies-to-lovers. COWBOY.

ME:

Gigi, there is not an HEA in my future.

GIGI:

You don't know. It could be fate.

ME:

No.

GIGI:

But you loved him once. This is your second chance romance, baby!

ME:

No.

GIGI:

I say you give him a ride around the ring before you decide. For old time's sake.

ME:

No.

GIGI:

You have to at least see if the chemistry is still there. For science.

ME:

You are impossible.

GIGI:

Why are you so against this? What do you have to lose?

GIGI:

Is it because of the other guy?

Which one?

GIGI:

Your lack of response confirms it. Sandwich time!

ME:

Leave me alone.

GIGI:

Listen, all I'm saying is you're living out the fantasy right now. You have every single romance trope all tied up in a bow. OMG, forced proximity! Now you just need one bed. Just . . . do your best to avoid accidental pregnancy, okay? Apparently, no one likes that anymore, according to social media.

GIGI:

Personally, the breeding kink is my jam. I love when the men get all growly and 'I'm gonna put my baby in you so you can never leave me.' And the pregnancy sex scenes *fans self* We love a man who knows how to take care of his woman. And who appreciates her no matter what shape she might be at the time. More, even, because she's carrying his child. *swoon*

GIGI:

I might have lost my original train of thought. *watches the train disappear in a sexy cloud of cowboy breeding smoke*

ME:

There will be no breeding.

Liar, liar. You loved it when Walker went bare.

GIGI:

Okay, but if there is, remember Gigi is a very solid name. It goes with everything.

ME:

I don't think my future son will be too excited about it.

GIGI:

He could be a little Gideon. Also, just G works fine.

ME:

Noted.

ME:

Wait . . . isn't Gideon Cross the hero in one of your favorite romance novels?

GIGI:

Maybe . . .

I couldn't help but smile. She was always able to cheer me up.

GIGI:

So if you're not gonna let him put a baby in you, are you getting divorced?

My stomach churned at her question.

ME:

I don't know.

GIGI:

Oh my God. You're still in love with him, aren't you? I knew you were holding out on me. I saw a picture of him. I see why you'd be swayed. They should put that man's face next to 'smolder' in the dictionary.

ME:

Pretentious might be a better place for it. Or taciturn.

GIGI:

Methinks the lady doth protest too much.

ME:

I see your Bard and raise you a Mel Brooks. Don't get saucy with me, bearnaise.

GIGI:

God, I miss you and your jokes about Willie Shakes.

GIGI:

But seriously, why no divorce?

ME:

It's complicated. I'm not rushing to the lawyer yet. But we're not in love. We barely tolerate each other.

GIGI:

Well, if I've learned anything from the 462 romance novels I read last year, sometimes all that not getting along is really just denial. Maybe stop trying so hard to convince yourself you're not still attracted to him. What's the worst that can happen? Hate sex? You know how hot hate sex can be.

ME:

And if we just hate each other?

GIGI:

Then my brother will be there in a couple of days and will put the bastard in his place. You know how much Bear loves to hand people their asses.

That was very true. Bear was scary to everyone but me and Gigi. To us, he was a teddy. To the rest of the world, he was a grizzly.

GIGI:

I've gotta head out. Inventory calls.

ME:

Thanks for being in my corner, G.

GIGI:

I'm in all your corners. Also, I throw a mean baby shower . . . you know, in case the breeding kink gets the better of you.

ME:

. . .

GIGI:

Love you!

As soon as our conversation was over, that light she'd brought to my day began to diminish, overcast by the shadow of my reality. There would be no hate sex. None. Zero. Zilch.

I stared at the portrait of Senior and narrowed my eyes. "No grandbabies from me. Don't get any more bright ideas."

My heart gave a little pang, and my frown grew. As much as I wanted to blame Senior for this, I couldn't forget the part my father played in this deception. How could he do that to me? He had to have a good reason. He wouldn't just sell me off like I was one of his prize cows. I was their only child, and neither of my parents treated me like anything other than their beloved daughter. My family had been beautiful and stable. So how had this happened?

Part of me wanted to trust that there was a bigger decision behind this. My dad must've known something I didn't. And Senior clearly hadn't been a man who made rash choices when it came to legally binding contracts.

I read the article Gigi had sent in her first message as my mind spun with all the reasons they might have had for this union. Unfortunately, no matter how long I thought about it, I remained no closer to an answer.

"Ugh!" I growled when I realized I'd lost another half hour to this stupid article. There was no way I was getting any work done today. I needed to go outside and clear my head. Maybe go for a swim. Or a ride.

I know someone who would love to take you for a ride.

That little voice in the back of my head sounded a lot like Gigi, but I didn't know who it meant.

Walker, Bishop, or Cross.

IN THE END, I chose a walk rather than any of my other options. I wanted the fresh morning air without the responsibility of taking care of an animal as I put my mind in order. So, dressed in boots and a flowy white sundress, I snagged a cowboy hat and set out to explore more of the ranch. There were structures all over the place, with dirt roads that reached beyond my line of sight. I guessed that was natural for the largest ranch in the state. With this much property, you'd need a lot of people and equipment to maintain it.

I spotted the shirtless man before I noticed the truck a few yards away, music floating out of its rolled-down window while he repaired a bit of fence. I couldn't keep myself from giggling when a horse moseyed from the other side of the fence and knocked his baseball cap off.

"Oh, that's real nice. I thought you were a lady," he grumbled good-naturedly as he bent down and rescued the hat.

The horse came after his hat again, but Bishop stopped her with a gentle hand, pulling a peppermint stick from his pocket.

"You know what they say about the way a man treats animals, right?" I said, approaching him slowly while doing my best not to drool because of all the muscles and sun-darkened skin on display. I didn't want to startle him, especially not after our conversation about how he got those scars.

He turned toward me, a grin on his lips. "I do not. Care to enlighten me?"

Well, shit. I wasn't sure where I'd been going with that. "Um . . . I actually don't think they say anything about them."

His eyes were knowing, but he didn't press me. He just peeled off his work gloves and came over to where I was standing. "What brings you all the way out here?"

"Needed to clear my head."

His gaze traveled across my face, lingering on my lips before returning to my eyes. "Husband troubles?"

"You could say that."

"Did you know he was going to announce it?"

My heart fluttered at the softness in his voice. He wasn't hurt or angry, just asking an honest question.

"No. But like you said, it's better this way, right? It gives me protection."

"He should've warned you, though. No one likes to be blindsided."

I snorted. "That's sort of Cross's MO."

"You deserve better than that. No wonder the prick has stayed single so long."

"Technically he hasn't."

"What do you think your husband's gonna say about us?"

"Can you stop calling him my husband?"

"That's what he is."

"No, he's my . . ."

"Cross to bear?"

There was something about the way he was looking at me, a light in his eyes that gave him away.

"Did you just make a joke?"

"C'mon, that was pretty good."

"I'll give you that." I laughed, my mood lightening like it had when I'd been chatting with Gigi. Then I sobered a little and answered his question. "Cross and I might be married, but I don't consider him my husband. A husband is someone you love, who takes care of you, builds a life beside you. All Cross has ever done was tear mine down. Even if I decide to stay in this stupid marriage like you suggested, it will take a lot more than a piece of paper and some signatures to make him my husband."

"Well, that's good to know."

"Why's that?"

He stepped closer to me, his gaze darkening as he gripped the brim of his hat and slid it around. The move was smooth and practiced, like he'd done it countless times before, but it made my belly swoop. Especially when he leaned in so his lips could hover over mine.

"Cause it would be a lot more complicated when I did this."

He kissed me softly. It was more a greeting than a seduction, but it lit a fire inside me anyway.

Bishop pulled away before I was ready, but I ignored the instinct to grab him and pull him back to me.

"What was that for?" I breathed.

"Do I need a reason to kiss you?"

"No."

"Good," he said, feathering his lips over mine again before grinning a little and admitting, "But I did it because I've been missing you, and you look really fucking pretty today, siren."

My cheeks burned under his attention, and my lips still tingled from his kiss. "Why'd you stop?"

"That was just a warm-up. Come here, beautiful. Let's see if I can't do something about that frown in your eyes."

He gripped me by the nape and yanked me against him, our bodies colliding as he brought his mouth to mine. This time it wasn't sweet or tender. It was a claiming, and I put up no resistance. Parting my lips, I welcomed his tongue as he walked us back until I was pressed against the side of the truck.

"I want to touch you, Sterling," I whispered against his mouth. "I want to make you feel good." I could feel how warm he was from spending hours in the sun, and I wanted to lick my way down his body. I didn't even mind that he was a little sweaty from his work. If anything, it only made me want to do it more. Honestly, I just wanted him.

His eyes darkened, and I braced myself for his rejection. But he surprised me.

"Tell me what you want to do."

"Taste you. Make you come. Make you feel the same way I did at the gala."

Gripping my hips, he twisted us so he was the one pressed against the truck now. The way his breaths came in harsh rasps told me two things: this was something he needed, but the touching part of it was going to be a challenge.

"No hands. Please. I can't . . ."

"I understand. You're the one in control, okay? If you need me to stop or change your mind, just say so, and I will."

"Usually that's my line." There was so much desire burning in his eyes, it felt like he could light me on fire with a single look.

Moving to drop to my knees, I offered him a grin, but he stopped me before I went to the ground.

"Wait, not yet." He reached into the truck's cab through the open window and brought out a wool blanket, handing it to me. "For your knees. I won't have you tearing them up out here."

"I wouldn't mind having reminders of you on my skin."

The way he groaned had my thighs clenching together, wetness flooding my center.

"Kneel, baby. I need your lips wrapped around me."

I laid out the blanket and did as I was told, loving the rough gravel in his command. Hands planted on my thighs, I waited for him to give me a taste, anticipation racing through my bloodstream.

I knew he was big after feeling him hard and needy against my belly at the gala. Not to mention the tented shorts I'd witnessed when he was lifting weights. But nothing prepared me for what I saw when he opened his fly and pulled himself free of those jeans.

Lord have mercy. Walker had shocked me with his piercing, but Sterling was going to ruin me with that beast between his legs. It was thick and veiny, large enough that I wasn't sure I could fit him in my mouth. The tip was deep red and already beaded with precum I wanted to lick clean.

"God, siren, you're looking at me like you've never sucked a cock before."

"I haven't."

He threaded his fingers in my hair and tugged until I looked up at him. "What did you just say?"

"I've never done this."

Confusion flickered over his face. "But . . ."

I knew he was trying to figure out how I could have been with both Cross and Walker without sucking a dick. "I sort of jumped over that part with Cross, and then after . . . I dunno, it's a vulnerability thing. Seems more intimate than sex to me, and I never felt safe enough or close enough with anyone else for us to get there."

"And you do with me?"

I nodded. "You make me feel like nothing can hurt me."

"We don't have to do this if you're not ready for it."

"I'm on my knees. I'm more ready than I've ever been. I love knowing you'll be my first. Just . . . teach me how to do it?"

A flare of possessive male pride flashed in his eyes as his fingers tightened in my hair. "Open for me, baby."

eight

. . .

Cross

"No one has time for your pity party, Walker. Answer my damn calls, or get your ass home. We've got shit to do," I snarled.

I scrolled through our text thread, unconsciously counting the unread messages I'd sent him since he'd stormed into the kitchen yesterday and dropped a marriage bomb.

ME:

If you're done being a pouty bitch, come meet me in the office. We need to discuss how we're going to handle the new round of shipments.

ME:

What the fuck am I paying you for if you can't be assed to participate in the business?

ME:

Don't fucking ignore me.

ME:

Walker. I swear if you knock some girl up because you're on a bender, you'll just prove Dad right. Don't do something stupid.

ME:

At least let me know you're alive and not in a ditch somewhere.

ME:

Goddammit, did you block me?

ME:

Real fucking mature.

ME:

You better be in a fuckin' hospital with two broken hands, you selfish asshole. Get the fuck over it and come home. No one has seen or heard from you since yesterday.

I'd sent that one as soon as I'd woken up this morning and saw he still hadn't checked his phone. Then in a fit of desperation, I'd added:

ME:

River deserves better from you.

Walker was a grown-ass man, but we had too many enemies for him to go MIA like this. It was irresponsible, not to mention fucking annoying. I knew his ego was bruised, but this was ridiculous, even for him.

Which was why I'd begun to worry.

Snagging my hat off the rack, I put it on and went to search for him. Maybe the idiot had made his way home but was ignoring us all. Or maybe he's still sleeping it off. If he was, I was about to haul his ass outside and hose him down.

I made my way to his bedroom, not bothering to knock before throwing the door open. Bed was still made, no sign of my brother.

Fuck. Where the hell are you, Walker?

Maybe he wasn't in his bed because he'd fallen into River's. That idea didn't sit right with me. Not now. Not ever, if I was being honest. I wanted to leave my mark on every fucking part of her, even the ones I had to share.

"We don't go no contact," I muttered as I continued down the hall. "Rule one. Always respond."

Three cowboys stood around the island in the kitchen we had just for the ranch hands. Each of them had a steaming mug of coffee in hand as they shot the shit, their sunbaked faces all smiles and jovial laughter. Part of me wanted to remind them of exactly what they'd been up to last night, of the battered and bloody man they'd left hog-tied naked in his barn. All of it on my order. Fucker was just lucky he was still breathing. No one stole from me and got away with it. It didn't matter if it was a single steer or an entire herd.

"Mornin', boss," Tex said, lifting his coffee cup in salute.

"Mornin'. You seen my brother?"

He gave a slow shake of his head. "Not since last night."

"We could'a used his help last night with the herd. He was supposed to join us," Russ offered.

"Rusty's just mad because he got on the wrong side of an angry heifer."

I frowned, ignoring that for now and zeroing in on Tex. "Where was he?"

"The Prospector, that little dive down by the freeway," he added when it was clear I didn't recognize the name.

"What was he doing at that shithole?"

"Drinkin'."

"Of fucking course he was," I muttered. "Was he upright when you left?"

Tex nodded. "He was planning on meeting up with us."

Russ snickered. "Guess he found someone prettier to roll around with instead."

"Or he drank himself under the table. He was three drinks deep by the time I left and looking a little worse for wear." Tex gave me a solemn look. "That man was nursing a serious case of heartbreak."

Heartbreak that was all my fault, even if it'd been without my knowledge. Well, initially. The headline I'd insisted on certainly couldn't have helped.

"Do me a favor?" I asked, glancing over at Rusty before pouring myself a thermos of coffee.

"Of course."

"Check to see if Blue is in the stable. I doubt he crawled home and took her out, but at this point, we need to search for him. Tex, you head to the bar and see if he's sleeping it off, will ya?"

Tex nodded, draining his coffee and heading out.

Russ eyed me. "And you? Are you going to look for him?"

That had been the plan before I'd learned his disappearing act had been due to drinking himself under a table. I hoped he woke up with a hangover from hell for worrying me like that. But now that I knew someone had at least had eyes on him, some of the urgency had ebbed, allowing me to focus on other matters.

"No. I need to have a talk with my wife."

THE LAST THING I expected to find when one of the new guys told me he'd spotted River walking in this direction was her on her knees with Bishop's dick halfway down her throat. But here we were.

"Jesus Christ," I groaned under my breath. I had to admit, she looked really fucking hot like that, with one exception. It wasn't my cock she was sucking or my hand in her hair.

From my angle, I was mostly behind her but just a bit to the right, so I could still catch glimpses of her face. Specifically the hollowing out of her cheeks and the way her eyes were currently squeezed shut. I also couldn't help but notice the way her fingers dug into her thighs.

"That's it, baby. Take it nice and deep. Goddamn, you feel good." Bishop's words were a harsh rasp, his head tilted back, eyes closed, fingers gripping her hair at the roots.

Lucky bastard.

I didn't have an excuse for why I was just standing there, watching like it was my own personal peep show, but I couldn't find it in me to move. Especially with how hard my own dick was. I adjusted myself on instinct, wishing I could tear her away from him and show her what she was missing, but that wouldn't help my cause one bit.

"Fuck, siren. You keep humming like that I'm gonna come down your throat."

Her head bobbed, a little whimpered moan escaping her that had my cock jerking. I took a step forward, and I must have stepped on a damn twig because Bishop's gaze shot my way. We were far enough apart that I couldn't read the expression in his eyes, but I had no difficulty interpreting the smug curl of his lips.

Fucker.

He didn't stop, just held my stare while River continued to suck him down.

"Look at you out here, on your knees where anyone could see you. Put your hand between your legs, baby. Touch your wet pussy and make yourself feel good."

She backed away from him, and to his credit, he let her. Hand holding her in place, he kept her from looking around. The man didn't want River to know I was here.

"Pull your skirt up and spread those thighs. I want to watch you get yourself off while I fuck your face."

The moan that left her was fucking obscene.

"Is that what you want? To be watched?"

I could stop this right now with a single word. Interrupt them before either of them found release. But I didn't. I was too invested in her answer.

"It depends on who's doing the watching," she said.

"Tug those panties to the side and show me how you glisten, beautiful. Show me what my cock in your mouth does to you."

As she obeyed, he kept on talking to her while he fed her his cock again.

"What do you think Cross would say if he saw you right now? His pretty wife, rubbing that greedy little clit and on her knees for me." It looked like she wanted to pull back and answer, but he held her in place and rocked into her some more. "I think he'd fucking love it. I think he'd wish it was him instead of me, but he wouldn't be able to look away long enough to do anything about it."

God, I wanted to see what she was doing. The way her hips bucked as she took him made me desperate to slide inside her heat and remind her what I could give her too. He could have her mouth. I'd claim that pussy. Again.

My sparrow made the sweetest sounds as she chased her release.

"Not yet, siren. Ride the edge for me. This is too perfect to rush." He pulled out of her mouth again, and she made a needy little noise.

"Why'd you stop me?"

"I have another question and want to hear your answer." He smirked down at her as she continued to work herself. "If your husband was here right now, what would you want? For him to try and take you from me or for him to join us?"

She paused, and he scolded her with a stern look.

"Keep rubbing that clit, siren. I didn't tell you to stop."

"O-okay. I'm just . . . so close."

Fuck, I was standing there, palming my hard dick, waiting with bated breath for her to say what she wanted. I couldn't leave now. Not until she answered.

"Tell me, and then we can get back to chasing that release."

"If he were here . . ."

I stopped fucking breathing.

"I'd want you both."

A heartbeat away from tearing open my fly, I gritted my teeth and worked for the control I so desperately needed. Until Bishop's eyes met mine again.

"What do you say, Mr. Cross? Are you going to give your wife what she's asking for?"

nine

. . .

Bishop

Fuck, River's mouth around my shaft was a heaven I hadn't realized I was missing, but when she looked up at me with those wide green eyes of hers and murmured, "I'd want you both." I was lost. I nearly came right then and there.

I wasn't much for sharing, at least I didn't think I was, but the idea of her body writhing between ours while we sent her over the edge was doing it for me in a big fucking way. Part of what I loved about ropes was having my partner at my mercy. Cross could hold her hands just as well as a rope or cuffs. My dick pulsed in my hand.

Oh, fuck yes.

Matching Cross's stare, I smirked and tightened my hold on River's long locks.

"What do you say, Mr. Cross? Are you going to give your wife what she's asking for?"

River jerked, her eyes wide when she realized my questions hadn't been hypothetical.

I held her in place. "Eyes on me, siren."

"Sterling—"

"Do you trust me?" I asked, voice low and only for her as Cross made his way over to us.

"Yes, but . . ."

"No buts. Do you trust me to take care of you and give you what you need? Even the things you're too scared to ask for?"

"Yes."

"That's my girl. I won't let him do anything to you that you don't want."

Cross's low growl had her turning her head to look at him. "I'm not going to touch her unless she asks for it."

"What do you say, baby? Do you want him to help you out? Or should he leave?"

She so clearly desired him. It was painted on her face. If I could give her that, make sure she felt safe while giving in to her hunger for the man who'd been her adversary for years, I would. I'd do fucking anything for her.

"Make me come, Cross," she whispered. "Make me come while I suck another man's dick."

There was just one last thing I needed to get out of the way first, just to ensure this didn't go terribly wrong for all of us.

"Cross."

He glared at me while moving into position behind River.

"Her only."

His brows furrowed until River whispered, "He doesn't like to be touched. It's a trigger."

"No worries there. I'm not interested in anything you have to offer, Bishop. It's only been her."

I gave him a sharp nod, and the man dropped to his knees behind River, hands splaying across her waist as though he was an explorer who had finally found the treasure he'd been searching for.

"Make her moan around my cock, Cross." I pressed the crown of my dick against her lips, but held back as Cross slipped one hand between her legs. "If it's too much, or you change your mind, squeeze my ankle and I'll stop."

Blinking up at me, she asked, "Are you sure?"

"Yes."

I was fucking trembling on the inside at the thought, but she needed a way to make me aware of her boundaries. It was too important.

She gave a little nod. "Okay, but I won't change my mind."

I smirked at her. "Open up, baby. Show me what you've learned."

A ragged moan left her as Cross did something between her legs, but I was too focused on how good it felt to slide my dick into her mouth to see it. That didn't stop me from catching him taking the end of the bow behind her neck and tugging on it until the top of her dress sagged and revealed a set of perfect fucking tits. I wanted to slide between them and fuck them until I came all over her.

Jesus.

I was so goddamn close.

"Look at you, taking his dick while I fuck you with my fingers. You're so damn wet for us. I can hear it every time I pump inside you."

She groaned, the vibration running over my length and making my balls draw up.

"Fuck, baby, do that again."

"You heard him, sparrow."

Her entire body shivered as he bit down on her neck. She loved being bossed around by both of us. Feeling both of us playing with her at the same time.

Cross cupped one breast with his free hand and rolled a tight pink nipple between his fingers, distracting her from the blow job she was giving me. She was overwhelmed; that much was clear, so I pulled out of her mouth and made her look at me.

"I'm going to do the work now. You don't come until I do, understand?"

She licked her lips and nodded.

I brushed my thumb down her cheek. "So fucking pretty when your lips are red and swollen like this."

Cross murmured his agreement, still kissing and biting his way along her shoulders and neck.

"Your little cunt is still so tight. Did you know that, sparrow? I can barely fit two fingers inside you. If I didn't know better, I'd think you were still a virgin. What about here?" His voice dropped, and she cried out and leaned back into him. "Has anyone taken you here yet?"

"No. No one."

"Another cherry for me to pop."

"Not if I get there first," I muttered.

"More, Cross. I need more."

"Fuck, I love the way you moan my name. Like you're dying for me."

"I hate you."

"I don't think you do. Not with the way you're soaking my fingers."

He pulled his hand away and sucked the digits clean while I slid the tip of my dick across her bottom lip, leaving a trail of precum in my wake. The way her tongue darted out to taste me had any hint of jealousy I felt toward Cross disappearing. She wanted me just as much. I was the one she'd given this first to. The one she'd given her *trust* to.

Holding her head where I wanted it, I thrust into her mouth. "Ready for me to fuck your face, baby?"

She made a happy humming sound that had my eyes nearly rolling back in my head.

"Suck him deep, sparrow. Then I'll make you come on my fingers like a good girl should."

I thrust into her in long rolls of my hips, sweat breaking out across my body as she swallowed around my thickness. Fuck, I needed to come. I wanted to feel her cry out around me as she followed me and the two of us left Cross with his metaphorical dick in his hand.

"Is she there, Cross?"

"I've had her on the edge all this fucking time. Are you ready to let her fall?"

"Fuck yes."

"Give it to me, sparrow. Sing for us."

I couldn't see, but I was guessing Cross added another finger because it felt like her entire body tightened and then went limp with relief as she toppled off the cliff and straight into her climax. Her moans were little more than sweet vibrations around my dick as I went with her, shooting jet after jet of my cum down her throat.

I didn't care that another man had made her climax while she sucked me off or that she was more than likely in love with the bastard, even if she wouldn't admit it to herself. All I wanted was for my girl to have every single thing she dreamed of, and this, right here, was proof I could. At least this dream.

There might be some others I couldn't ever give her. Like the freedom to touch me the way she wanted to. A normal life. A picket fence.

I could barely stand the thought of holding her hand without breaking into a sweat.

Maybe sharing her was the perfect solution. Even if the men I'd be sharing with were the same ones I was supposed to help put behind bars.

But as River blinked up at me with that sated look in her green eyes, I couldn't find it in myself to worry about the future.

She was happy. That was enough for now.

ten

• • •

River

I could still feel the pulse of Bishop's cock as he came down my throat, the scrape of Cross's stubble along my neck and shoulder, the burn deep inside as his fingers stretched me. Not to mention the little flutters that accompanied those memories, like my very own ghost of the orgasm he'd given me.

Great, my vagina's haunted. Gigi will be so proud.

I dropped my forehead on my vanity with a groan. I'd been doing so well resisting Cross—if avoiding him was the same as resisting. But all it took was a little voyeurism and Bishop bossing me around, and I was right back where I'd been at eighteen.

You can't blame Sterling. He gave you an out. You were the one who begged for it.

"Ugh," I groaned again, this time banging my head gently on the desk. "Stupid. Stupid. Stupid."

Imagine what it'd be like with Walker in the mix. Three men . . . three holes. You'd probably die. That thought came through loud and clear in my best friend's voice. Gigi might swallow her tongue when I told her about this. Or name me her patron saint and light a candle in my honor.

Although Walker'd been completely silent on all fronts since he'd shared the joyous nuptial news with all of us. I hadn't done myself any favors with him, though. There was nothing like a crushing rejection to send a man away with his tail between his legs.

God, when he found out about this . . . he'd never forgive me. Knowing I let his brother fingerblast me while sucking Bishop's dick right there where anyone could find us. Not even a day after I told him I was choosing myself over all of them? Oh my God, I was a terrible human. He didn't deserve this. He'd treated me like I was something precious and to be protected. I turned around and made a sandwich with everyone but him.

Technically, I hadn't done anything wrong. I hadn't made any promises, which meant I couldn't break one. But knowing that didn't do a thing for my guilt.

This was a real pickle, as my mama used to say. And I didn't know how to get out of it. I needed to stay married to Cross for a multitude of reasons, but the big one was a gigantic Russian who apparently didn't take no for an answer.

I sent a text to Walker, hoping he'd answer me now that he'd had time to cool off.

ME:

I'm sorry for how we left things. Can we talk?

When he didn't immediately answer, I sighed and dropped my phone. He was probably giving me a taste of my own medicine. Fair enough. I was bound to run into him sooner or later. This place was massive, but it was still one building. I could wait. Maybe come up with a better explanation for what happened than how I tripped and fell to my knees, but thankfully Bishop was there, and he caught me with his dick. And then Cross tripped, and his hands just happened to tear my dress off and slide right inside me with no help from either of us.

My life was officially a porno. Cue the bad seventies music.

A sharp knock on my door had me on my feet and rushing to answer. Tearing open the door, I breathed, "Walker, I'm—"

Except it wasn't Walker standing in my doorway, it was Cross. Cross, who'd touched me and left beard burn on my skin. Who'd made me come so hard I saw stars and wished he'd do it all over again, but this time with his big cock.

Jesus. Pull yourself together, River.

"What do you want?" I snapped.

He was too busy devouring me with his eyes to register my tone. "I'm here to take you to dinner."

"I'm not hungry," I said, starting to close the door in his face.

He stopped me with a boot. "I'm not asking."

"You're impossible."

"And you still taste like fucking candy, sparrow." The way his voice rolled over me sent goosebumps across my flesh.

"Stop it."

"Stop what?"

"Flirting with me."

"You're my wife. I can flirt if I want."

I shot him a glare. "I'm your wife now?"

He leaned against the doorframe. "According to that piece of paper, you have been for ten years."

"A piece of paper isn't shit, Cross. You've done nothing but try to make me miserable since I arrived."

"Sounds like every marriage I've ever heard of."

"Well, you don't have a great example to go by. I want the kind of love my parents had, and—"

"You don't think that's possible with me."

"If the love letter I still have memorized is anything to go by, no."

He winced. "You don't understand."

"Don't I? Allow me to recite it for you, and you can clarify what I don't understand."

He reached out and put his fingers over my mouth before I could start. "You are so fucking stubborn."

"You're just mad because I'm right," I said, my lips rubbing against the fingers that were inside me hours earlier. I was still dick-drunk enough to want to suck them into my mouth. Or bite them off.

"I was young and dumb."

"Still are the latter."

He gritted his teeth, but I saw the flicker of amusement in his eyes. "Come. Eat. Supper's on the table."

I raised a brow. "Is it the corpse of your latest victim? Because I think I'm vegan now."

"Watch it."

"Or what?"

He glared at me, all sorts of wicked promises in his gaze, and fuck if they didn't make me tingle. This was all Bishop's fault. He opened Pandora's box, and now I was a filthy whore.

"Don't make me toss you over my shoulder, River."

He'd do it. No question.

I huffed but grabbed my phone and tucked it into the pocket of my jeans—my poor sundress was ruined, and I'd had to change the second I got back to my room. "Fine. Lead the way."

He didn't speak, simply took me by the hand and tugged me out of my room and down the hall. Instead of turning toward the kitchen where we'd taken most of our meals, he went the opposite direction toward the formal dining room. I hadn't been in here since our families last shared Christmas together.

Tonight the table was set with two place settings directly across from each other, a few candles flickering between the plates covered with silver domes.

"You really went all out."

"You're my wife."

"You keep saying that like it's an explanation."

"Isn't it?"

I shook my head, not wanting to get back on that ride just yet. I was too curious what he'd made us for dinner.

He didn't make it. The chef did. Don't go getting heart eyes for the bastard now. He's playing you. Trying to butter you up. Don't be a bread roll, River! You're smarter than this.

He walked me to my chair, pulling it out and lightly touching my back as I sat.

Before I could say anything, he pulled the dome off my plate. A little breath escaped me.

Consider yourself buttered.

It was a plate of my favorites. Instead of steak and risotto or something equally fancy, it was loaded with mac 'n cheese and tater tots. Granted, they were homemade, and it looked like there might be bacon and perhaps chives in the tots, but they were still my favorites.

"Are you serious?"

A slight smirk twisted up his lips. "The last time I had to make you dinner, this was what you ate."

"I was twelve."

"I can send it back." He reached for my plate.

"No!" I slapped his hand away. Blushing furiously, I grumbled, "You forgot the dino chicken nuggets."

"Such a mature palate."

"Bite me."

That fucker did, right on the side of my neck. "Mmm, maybe we skip the dinner, and I can eat you instead. You'd look so good spread out on the table for me."

I shivered. "No. Just because you made me come doesn't mean you have full access to me whenever you want it."

"Maybe you should tell that to your cunt. Pretty sure she's weeping for me right now."

"Sit down and eat your mac 'n cheese."

One brow lifted as he took his seat across from me and lifted the lid on his, revealing . . . not mac 'n cheese.

"I'm sorry, what the fuck is that?"

I stared dubiously at the plate of steamed vegetables and . . . salmon?

"You call yourself a rancher."

"I am a rancher."

I gestured to the plate. "And you went with fish?"

"I like it."

"I don't even know who you are, Daniel Cross Jr."

"Clearly."

My phone chirped from my pocket, saving me from the staring contest happening between me and the smoke show that was the man I'd apparently married. Glancing down at the screen, I smiled at the message.

STERLING:

I can't stop thinking about how pretty you looked today.

Well, that was damn sweet. Unless he was thinking about what I looked like with my lips wrapped around his cock.

Knowing it would annoy my dinner companion, I texted back.

ME:

I bet you say that to all the girls.

"Who's that?" Cross asked, a rumble of disapproval in his tone.

"Why do you care?"

"If someone's gonna make you smile like that, I want to know who it is."

STERLING:

Never. Not once. It's only you, baby.

Shit. My cheeks were surely bright pink if the heat creeping up them was any indication.

"Who is that, sparrow?"

"Bishop."

He heaved a sigh, and something like disappointment crossed his perfect features.

"Jealous?"

"Yes."

"It's not like I'm keeping him a secret."

"Honestly, I'd hoped it was Walker."

"You haven't heard from him either?"

He shook his head and gestured at my plate with his fork. "Eat."

"And if I don't? You gonna send me to my room without dessert, Daddy?"

His eyes blazed. "After I tan your hide for that sassy mouth of yours."

Well, okay then.

I cleared my throat and scooped up a big bite. But before I could enjoy it, my phone went off again.

"Silence it or I'm taking it."

"You are so bossy."

He blinked at me.

Setting my fork down, I made a big show of lifting my phone so I could text Bishop back, but my blood ran cold at the message on the screen.

UNKNOWN:

I left you a present.

Underneath the message was a photo of Walker, unconscious, badly beaten, and slumped over in the dirt in front of the gates to Twisted Cross Ranch.

eleven

• • •

Cross

All the color drained from River's face as she stared down at her phone. I'd almost take the heat in her eyes when Bishop texted her over this. This was something bad, and apprehension hummed in my blood.

"Sparrow?"

She made a series of noises, like she was searching for words but couldn't come up with any. Eventually she just slid her phone over to me.

"Fuck, Walker," I breathed, taking in the sight of my little brother's unconscious form. I was already on my feet, fury pumping through my veins. "Who sent you this?"

"I-I don't know."

A name didn't really matter. I already knew who was behind this. It had Dom's signature all over it. The bastard loved his messages to be bloody, bordering on lethal. But why send it to her instead of me? Or was this just another way of proving he could get me through both of them?

"Stay here," I ordered, keeping her phone in hand as I stormed out of the dining room and made a beeline for the front door.

"The hell I will!" she shouted, chasing after me. "Give me my damn phone, Cross."

Bishop was just coming into the house, a pizza box in one hand and a six-pack of beer in the other. "What the hell is going on?"

"You didn't fucking see Walker out there? You're clearly just getting back from town. Jesus, did you just leave him at the gate like that?" I knew Bishop didn't like people much, but I never thought he'd leave someone for dead. Especially after he made a point to stitch Walker up the last time.

"What do you mean? There wasn't anyone at the gate when I pulled in."

"They must've just left him. That's good, right? He hasn't been there long, then." River grabbed my hand, a surprising gesture I didn't have time to examine.

"Who knows how long they had him before they dumped him. He could have been bleeding out for hours already."

"Christ," Bishop muttered, dumping his dinner on the floor and racing toward his truck. "I'll drive."

I didn't fight him on it. The three of us piled in, River sandwiched between us though she was careful to leave a sliver of space between her and him. We were all tense as Bishop started the engine, and we headed down the long driveway. God, why was it such a long distance from the house to the gate? In theory, the privacy was great, but damn, right now I wished we were already there.

Dust flew up all around us as Bishop sped down the drive. I didn't even want to know how fast he was going; I just appreciated the hustle. As the gate came into view, he didn't slow so much as fishtail, tires squealing as they fought for purchase on the pavement. The truck was still on as we jumped out, lights pointed at the gate and illuminating the heap that was my brother.

"Walker!" I shouted, hoping he'd give us some sign he was still breathing.

The gate opened as we approached, the heavy metal panels rolling to the sides far too slowly for my liking. River was on Walker as soon as she could get through, her hands hovering over his battered face like she didn't know where to touch him.

"Jesus," she whispered.

Part of me expected her to dissolve into tears, but seeing how badly he was injured seemed to have the opposite effect. She was clearly upset, but she shoved her feelings aside so she could deal with the situation. It made me wonder just what her life had been like in Alaska. Her cool efficiency was not a normal reaction to seeing torture victims for the first time.

"I can't tell where he's hurt the worst." She glanced up at me, her eyes wide but voice steady.

"Is he breathing?" Bishop asked.

The big ranch hand stood apart from us, brows pulled together, hands clenched into fists. He seemed to be struggling.

"Yes," River said, putting two fingers on his neck as she checked his pulse. "His pulse is steady too."

One of his legs was at an odd angle, telling me it was broken. There wasn't a whole lot of him that wasn't covered in blood or bruises, but his legs seemed to be the worst of it. At least in terms of the injuries we could see.

"Are those burns?" I asked, crouching down to get a better look at the charred patches of skin on the bottom of his feet.

"Blowtorch," Bishop supplied, his voice rough.

"How can you tell?" River asked.

"Trust me."

"You've seen this before?" I asked.

Bishop nodded, which only raised more questions, but he wasn't my problem right now. Getting my brother inside and tended to was.

"We need to get him into the truck and take him home."

"No. We need to take him to a hospital. Look at him. He's been tortured, Cross. He needs antibiotics, probably an MRI, or at least an x-ray. You can't do that at home."

"The doc can be here in ten minutes. If he says Walker needs more care, we'll take him in."

River got in my face, her expression furious. "If he dies because of your stupid need for secrecy, I swear to you I will make your life hell for the rest of your days."

I huffed. "Aren't you already doing that?"

I regretted the words as soon as I said them. I was supposed to be winning her over, not pissing her off, but worry for my brother was getting in the way of all my good intentions.

"Bishop, call Carter."

He didn't respond; his eyes were still glued to Walker's feet.

"Bishop?"

River stood and crossed the drive to reach him, cautious, careful, and gentle. "Sterling, it's okay."

She reached out, but didn't lay a hand on him. The man sucked in a tight breath and caught her by the wrist. The move was fast, but I caught the tremble in his fingers before they wrapped around her skin.

"Don't," he warned. "I just need a minute."

Understanding dawned. His aversion to touch. His skill set. I'd known he was ex-military; I just hadn't realized he suffered PTSD from his time overseas. It made sense, though. A lot of our guys had baggage they dealt with in silence. Ranching and working for Twisted Cross was, for the most part, a way to avoid the real world and keep to yourself unless we called you in. We'd been doing a hell of a lot more calling than usual lately.

"Sparrow, take my phone. Call Carter, tell him what happened and to meet us at the lodge." I handed her my cell and then glanced at Bishop. "You good to drive?"

He gave a tight nod and moved to Walker. "I'll get his shoulders."

Together we picked up my brother and carried him to the truck bed.

River made the call, but I wasn't paying attention to what she said as we worked together to keep him steady as we lifted him into the back. He was still out cold, which was probably a mercy, all things considered. He was going to be in a hell of a lot of pain once he regained consciousness.

"Fucking Russian assholes," I muttered under my breath as I settled in next to him. River tried to climb in on his other side, but I stopped her with a glare and a harsh, "No. You ride up front."

"But—"

"He's right. Come on, siren."

She wanted to fight us on it, and had I been the only one denying her, she might have. But Bishop must have been a River-whisperer because she gave a grumpy nod and went back around to the passenger side.

Walker let out a soft groan as the truck began moving, his eyes fluttering but never fully opening.

"It's okay, Walker. We got you. You're gonna be fine." I wasn't sure if that was the truth, but I didn't know what else to say. "We'll get you patched up as soon as Carter gets here. Then I'll make those bastards wish they'd never been born."

I didn't care who Dominik Volkov was or what promises my father made. No one fucked with my family and got away with it. As of this moment, all ties between Volkov International and Cross Industries were severed. No matter what that meant for my future.

Volkov wanted a war? He just got himself one.

And it was going to be fucking bloody.

Just like the last time.

Ten years earlier

RIVER WAS ALL I could think about as I drove out to meet my father and Casey Adams in the goddamn middle of the night. I should be asleep with her in my arms, letting myself be happy for once in my fucking life. Instead, we had an emergency on our damn hands, and it was messy. Of fucking course it was.

The type of mess remained to be seen. All I'd been told was something was wrong with one of the shipments and we had to get our asses down to the warehouse immediately. Given the types of goods we ran, that could really mean anything. We could be off weight. We could be missing product. We could have too much product. If it was one of our legit shipments, product could have spoiled.

My gut told me it was none of those things. We didn't even have anything scheduled to go out this late, and if there was a mechanical issue, that sure as shit wouldn't require my help.

I adjusted the gun strapped to my side, knowing full well I may need to use it tonight.

I knew as soon as we pulled up to the industrial building that something was very fucking wrong. We weren't greeted by security at the gate. All the floodlights were off. Not a single night guard or worker was in sight.

But there was blood. Splatters of it on the pavement, streaks smeared on the side of the building.

My dad pulled his gun and clicked off the safety as soon as he saw it, prompting Casey and me to do the same. Senior lifted a finger to his lips, as if I needed to be fucking told to stay silent. Heart in my throat, I followed around the building to the loading dock, hoping I wouldn't find what I expected.

One of our trucks was there, the ramp lowered as if someone had taken a break in the middle of loading or unloading.

"What the fuck is that smell?" Casey asked, disgust coating the question.

"Urine." Dad's answer might have been one word, but it hung there, heavy and ominous.

But that wasn't the worst of it. I'd caught the scent of copper on the wind. Thick, like you'd expect to find at the slaughterhouse. Not out here where everything should be neat and carefully packaged.

"Why would there be piss out here? We don't ship live animals." An overwhelming sense of dread hit me hard.

"It's not cows, son."

Senior pulled out his flashlight and turned it on, the bright beam washing over the loading dock.

"Jesus fucking Christ," Casey breathed.

A tidy line of bodies went from the truck all the way into the warehouse. Innocent people who I recognized as employees mixed in with a few of our ranch hands and guards.

"Is that Vic?" Casey asked, moving closer.

"Shit," my father cursed.

"Who the fuck would do this over cargo?" I asked, closing in on the open truck and covering my nose with the inside of my elbow as the stench grew stronger. "What were they after?"

"It looks to me like this wasn't our usual shipment." Casey pointed his flashlight inside the shipping container.

A horror show was the only way to describe it once I realized what I was looking at. I took a few running steps away and lost the contents of my stomach, gun clattering to the ground as I rested my hands on my knees.

People. People had been in that truck.

Some hadn't made it out alive. By the state of their bodies, they'd been dead long before they arrived at the warehouse, their wrists bound in front of them, tattered clothes stained and soiled.

Pulling myself together, I turned on my dad. "You're letting them ship humans? I knew you weren't the squeaky clean cowboy you pretend to be, but this is . . . I can't be part of this. Fuck, Dad, what would Mama think of you if she could see this?"

He shook his head, his face pale, eyes pleading. "I didn't know."

"The hell you didn't. Nothing goes on in this company without your okay. I can turn a blind eye to the drugs, and I can get behind the weapons, but this? *This* is the great Cross legacy? You are a sick bastard."

"On your mother's life, I didn't know." Senior stared me in the eyes, sincerity written on every word he said. "They told me it was a different type of cargo, but never this. I wouldn't have okayed it. Nothing is worth being part of something so wrong. Even a corrupt man has morals. This is a line I would never cross."

"It ends here," Casey said. "Look at what your negligence has already cost us. These were good people. Mothers, daughters, husbands, sons. What happens when they come even closer and take out everyone who matters to us? You think Luca's just going to let us walk away from this now that he got what he wanted? The Russians don't work like that."

Senior hung his head. "What do you want me to say? I fucked up, okay? I thought it would be the normal deal. I grease a couple of palms and let them use our trucks, no questions asked. How was I supposed to know this is what they wanted to use it for?"

"Luca has a reputation for trafficking. Girls. Pretty young girls who fetch him a lot of money. Did you really not even consider that was his 'special' cargo?"

Casey was angrier than I'd ever seen him. I couldn't remember a time he and my dad had ever fought like this in front of me.

"What does he have on you, Daniel? That's the only reason you'd do this."

Senior shook his head, unable to look his friend in the eye. "I can't tell you that."

"Goddammit, you played right into his hand. He's not gonna stop with this massacre. Do you know what he told me when I saw him at the club last week, D? He said, 'That little one of yours has certainly ripened nicely.' Then he offered to take her off my hands."

The last bit Casey said to me. I'm almost positive he intended for his words to be some sort of appeal, as if I needed a reason to take his side in this argument. What he couldn't have known was how deeply they'd affect me. That they'd be the verbal equivalent of a red flag waved in front of a bull. But that's exactly what they were.

I didn't know Luca Volkov personally, but his reputation preceded him. He made a killing selling heroin here in the States, but his real power came from the flesh trade. Porn. Prostitution. Blackmail. Many were politicians that got caught with their pants down with one of his underage girls. Luca was one of the most powerful men in the country, and he wasn't even American. There were whispers his nephew was being groomed to inherit his empire and that Dominik was just as ruthless as his godfather.

I was struck by the image of River at the mercy of that monster. The thought of what he might do to her had my stomach threatening to crawl up my throat.

Fury and revulsion collided within me, along with a healthy dose of desperation. We had to spare River from that fate. Or any that might place her in his crosshairs. "You have to send her away, Case. She can't be here, not if he's got his eye on her."

I don't know how I did it, but I managed to keep my voice from shaking. Luca couldn't be allowed to put his hands on her. Ever. I hated that he'd even noticed her.

Casey's gaze returned to my father, the two of them sharing a look I couldn't decipher. "She just turned eighteen. She's got her whole life ahead of her. I can't ruin it by making her leave."

The last thing I wanted was to lose my sparrow now, but this right here was proof she wasn't safe. "Get her out of here. She needs to be protected, and we clearly can't do that."

My father and Casey exchanged another look and this time Senior shrugged, as if to say the choice was up to him. Why the hell was Casey looking to him for guidance—or was it permission?—about what to do with his own daughter?

"We'll bring her back once it's safe, Case. Don't worry," Senior promised.

Finally, Casey let out a heavy sigh and nodded. "You're right. I'll send her—"

I shook my head. "Don't tell us. It's better if we don't know."

And there'd be less temptation for me to follow her and ruin her life.

"Things will work out just as we planned. We just need to deal with this first," Senior said, clapping his friend on the shoulder.

Casey flinched away, rage in his eyes. "It might never be over. Not with these assholes."

Not one to be dissuaded, my dad slung his arm around Casey's shoulder, voice dripping with steely determination, "Then I just have to make sure I come up with a permanent solution. I'll handle the Russians. You take care of your daughter."

It was the only plan that would keep her out of harm's way. Unfortunately, for it to be successful, I'd have to break her heart—and mine.

twelve

. . .

Walker

Three days later

"Sonofabitch," I hissed, eyes narrowed into slits. Even breathing fucking hurt. Scratch that; breathing especially fucking hurt. It felt like tiny knives stabbed my lungs with each inhale.

"Careful. Don't try and sit up."

River's warning voice was almost as jarring as the light. But it wasn't pain I felt at hearing it; it was relief.

"Ladybug?"

"Do you need anything? More meds?"

I wanted to pretend I was fine and that she was making a mountain out of a molehill, but I couldn't. This was bad. I hadn't hurt like this since that time I stole my dad's motorcycle and took it for a joyride but ended up losing control and crashing in a ditch.

"How long have I been out?" I rasped.

"On and off for the better part of three days. The doctor said you might be a little woozy and have some trouble remembering what happened." She said the last bit almost like it was a question. Like she wanted to ask, but also didn't.

I remembered all too well. My gut clenched at the phantom sound of a blowtorch igniting, but I pushed it away, not ready to relive any of it.

"I'm so glad you're alive. We almost lost you, Walker. I can't keep doing this."

"I thought you weren't. You chose you, right? You aren't obligated to be at my bedside."

Even though the light was dim, it was agony, but I forced my eyes wide open so I could really look at her. I knew I must look rough, given how I was feeling, but she seemed as if she was in as much pain as I was.

"I said a lot of things."

With all the strength I could muster, I reached out for her, the pain in my ribs almost unbearable. "So did I. I'm sorry for being so angry about Cross, River. I know this is an impossible situation and not something you did to hurt me. But I can't help falling in love with you, and I won't apologize for that. Even if you end up leaving us all, I won't stop loving you."

Pain had a surprising way of offering clarity, and my brush with death had made a few things abundantly clear. None of us knew how much time we had on this earth. It could be a lifetime; it could be a handful of days. Either way, I wanted to spend the time I had left with her. Whatever that looked like, I wanted in. She was it for me, even if I couldn't be it for her.

"Walker . . ." She sat on the side of the bed, so carefully I wondered if she thought she'd break me all over again. "I don't need you to apologize. You're allowed to be upset by this. But we don't have to talk about our situation right now. You need to recover first."

I took her hand, and just that small touch eased something inside me. She soothed my weary soul even without knowing it. God, I wanted her to love me back. I wanted it with everything in me, but I couldn't rush her. Thinking I'd up and marry her so soon after she came back to us had been cocky and overconfident, to say the least.

"I don't want to lose you, darlin'. Not to my brother, or to my own stubbornness. I'll wait as long as I have to for you to let me back in."

She stared down at me with nothing but affection in her eyes as she brushed the hair back from my forehead. "You're not gonna lose me."

"So you're telling me all I had to do was nearly die to get back in your good graces? As far as grand gestures go, that seems—"

A knock at the door interrupted the moment.

"Siren?"

"Come in," she called softly, pulling away from me and angling her body toward our visitor. I missed her touch instantly.

"I brought you something to eat, baby," Bishop cracked the door and peered in, catching a glimpse of me and stopping. "Oh, you're awake." He hovered as if second-guessing whether or not to step inside.

"S'all right," I said, proud of myself for being so damn magnanimous. Also, pretty sure those pain meds were kicking in.

"Just wanted to see how you two were doing and bring up some lunch." His eyes raked over her, and there was no masking the feelings there. He was as gone for her as I was. Clearing his throat, he glanced at me, explaining, "The only way we can get her to eat anything is to force the issue. She hasn't left your side. Not even to sleep or shower."

"That explains the smell."

"Walker!"

I chuckled and then winced. "Kidding."

"If anyone stinks, it's you," she said with a huff.

"What, you haven't been giving me sponge baths? What kind of nurse are you?"

"The kind who has been out of her mind with worry."

I stretched my arm out, palm up, and wriggled my fingers. She recognized the request for what it was and linked her fingers with mine. "Don't worry, darlin', you're still the prettiest woman I've ever seen. Terrible bedside manner or not."

Her eyes misted with tears, but she blinked them away. "You are so lucky you're hurt, or I'd smack you with a pillow, Walker Wayne."

"Shhh, we don't say that name out loud."

Bishop let out a rare laugh. "I see he's been given his latest dose of meds. Has he started reciting limericks yet? That was my favorite."

"No poems," River said.

"There once was a lady named Sally . . ."

Her eyes brightened, amusement sparkling in their depths, so I continued.

"Who lived at the end of an alley . . ."

"Okay, funny guy, that's enough. You need to go back to sleep. You're so beat up it hurts me to see you moving at all."

To be fair, it was a herculean task just keeping my eyes open, but I was afraid of what would be waiting for me if I closed them. Worse, I was afraid I'd wake up and find out this was all a dream. That my ladybug wasn't sitting at my bedside, worried about me, caring for me. Maybe even loving me . . .

Fuck.

"You never did say what the damage was. I'm guessing some broken ribs, and I can't move my legs. I know I'm not paralyzed, blood flow is working just fine, so . . ."

River blushed when I caught her eyes darting to my lap. I wriggled my eyebrows. "Don't believe me? I can prove it."

"I'm sure you can."

I yawned despite myself, and even that wasn't too comfortable.

"You've got four broken ribs, your jaw was dislocated, and your tibia was broken so badly you needed surgery to fix it," River said, her tone serious. Her gaze flicked to Bishop, then returned to me. "And you have some burns."

"My feet," I said, trying to keep my voice even. It's sort of hard to forget a blowtorch anywhere on the body. Thank the Lord they stopped there.

She bit her lip and nodded. "You're going to be in a wheelchair for a little bit until the skin heals. Then you can swap to crutches until your cast is ready to come off."

Jesus.

"A wheelchair?"

"Unless you want me to carry you everywhere, and something tells me you don't." Bishop crossed his arms over his chest. "Your brother is already working on setting up the main floor guest room for you so you can get around."

I groaned. "How am I supposed to win you back when I'm trapped in a chair?"

River made a soft sound and then cleared her throat. "Oh, I dunno, Walker. Pretty sure you'll find all kinds of reasons to take me for a ride."

My lips twitched up. I knew what she was doing. Flirting to try and make me feel better. It might even be working. "That was a pretty good line."

"I'm a little disappointed you missed it."

"Me too. I'm glad one of us is on our game."

"I'm heading out to check fence for a few hours, siren. Call me if you need me for any reason, okay?" Bishop came over and dropped a kiss to her forehead before leaving the two of us alone, but even if he hadn't made it as obvious as a sledgehammer to the face, I recognized the look in his eyes.

"He's in love with you."

She shook her head. "No. But there is something between us."

"Yeah, that's clear. And my brother? What about him?"

"It's complicated."

"He's your husband."

"Legally."

My eyes swept across her face, reading all the clues I'd spent my childhood learning. "If that's all it was, you wouldn't be blushing. You've loved him for as long as you knew what love was. That's not something you can just turn off. Trust me, I know."

"I don't want to choose between any of you."

"So don't."

"Are you serious?"

Blame the meds, blame the injuries, but I was feeling brave and a little desperate to hold on to her. "As long as I'm part of this puzzle, I'm fine with sharing you. I've had to my whole life anyway. What's one more heart in the mix? Just say you're mine too. That's all I need."

"I . . ." She blew out a breath. "We'll talk about this when you aren't medicated. I'm not fit to be making any promises right now. And you aren't either."

Another yawn took hold, and my blinks became longer and longer as exhaustion won out.

Her lips whispered across my forehead. "Get some sleep."

I couldn't get my eyes back open, but I could feel the air shifting around me as she pulled away. "Don't leave. Please."

"I'm not going anywhere, Walk. I'll be right here when you wake up, promise."

"I love you, ladybug. Always."

Her fingers trailed over my forehead and through my hair, probably the only part of me not injured at this point.

"I love you too, Walker Cross. I'm sorry it took me so long to realize it."

I was already drifting off and couldn't be sure her whispered confession was real or just a pain-induced fantasy.

But I clung to it anyway. Just like I was going to cling to her.

thirteen

. . .

River

Two days later

"Oh no, you don't. Walker Cross, get your ass back in bed this minute," I hollered as soon as I stepped out of the bathroom and found the stubborn cowboy trying to swing his legs over the side of his bed.

"I need to take a leak."

"That's what the—"

"I swear to God, woman, if you try and talk to me about the fucking piss bucket one more time."

"It could be the catheter."

"That inhumane piece of plastic isn't going anywhere near my dick ever again."

His glare was accusatory. As if I should have stopped the doctor from doing his job. Who knew Cock Bodyguard was part of my job description?

"You don't complain about the sponge baths."

"That's different. Especially since you're doing that for me."

"If you need me to hold your dick for you while you're peeing, I'm out. Your arms work just fine."

"Aw, don't be like that. You sure seemed like you wanted to wrap your lips around it last time you two were up close and personal."

"Yeah, sure, but not when you're peeing!"

His sexy smirk dimmed. "This is really taking a sorry turn."

"At least take your meds? I know you've been holding off."

The man tried to hide the pain, but I could see it in the tightness around his eyes and mouth. Not to mention the beads of sweat dotting his brow. "I'm fine."

"Liar."

"I said I'm fine, dammit. Now help me or get the fuck out of my way."

I blew out a frustrated breath. I knew he was hurting, and for a tough guy like him, admitting he needed help was akin to sticking pins beneath his fingernails. That didn't mean I had to tolerate him treating me like a punching bag.

"You can't even walk."

"Then get my damn wheelchair."

"What I'm going to get is your brother."

He lifted his hands and mimed being afraid. "Oooh, no. Not the big bad Cross. I'm so scared."

"I don't want you to be scared. I want you to listen to reason, and apparently you've got your River filter on. Also, I can't lift you when you inevitably fall on your face and injure yourself again."

I pulled my phone from my pocket and texted Cross for the third time today, but just like the other two times, he didn't answer. So I sent him a string of messages, all with no response.

"Where are you?" I muttered. I knew he was here; his truck hadn't left the driveway since Walker was hurt.

Walker sighed. "Just give me the bucket, woman. But do me a favor and leave me alone for a few minutes. I need to preserve what little dignity I still have."

I bit down on my lip but nodded. As much as I didn't want to leave in case something happened, this would give me a chance to hunt his brother down. Walker was getting ornery. I wouldn't be able to manage him for much longer. Especially while he was still upstairs. Time to pull out the bigger, scarier guns.

I just needed the scarier gun to answer my fucking messages.

As soon as I was out of the room, I turned my attention to finding Cross. We needed to have a little chat about Walker management, and he wouldn't be able to ignore me if we were face to face.

With all the elegance of an angry bull, I barreled into Cross's bedroom, not giving two shits about things like knocking or privacy. *I mean, if it's good for the goose . . .*

"Don't you dare ignore my texts!"

Instead of finding a surprised cowboy, there was a whole lot of nothing waiting for me. I grunted and made to leave when I registered the shower running.

Well, that was just peachy. I'm over here still wearing the same clothes I slept in three days ago, and he's taking a luxurious shower. Fuck that.

"Where do you get off—" I started as I burst into the bathroom, but the words caught in my throat at the sight of Cross standing in the shower stall.

It was one of those open shower situations, with stonework from floor to ceiling. Jesus, the man's ass was a work of art. Even I could admit it. But the thing that really caught my attention wasn't his muscular form or the way his arm was braced on the wall in front of him. No, it was the long, slow glides of his hand over his fully erect dick that had me swallowing my words.

Apparently Cross gets off in the shower.

I was too shocked to move. I just stood there with my mouth hanging open.

He slowly turned his head and looked at me. "You just gonna stand there, or . . ."

He let the invitation hang, his strokes continuing at the same measured pace as if I wasn't even there.

"I . . . uh . . . are you . . ." I couldn't seem to form a coherent sentence. Great job, River. Way to be a good feminist and lose the power of speech at the sight of a big dick.

A big, sexy, slippery dick. That I wanted inside me.

Jesus.

"I'm fucking busy, sparrow. In case you haven't noticed."

"Then hurry up and finish so we can talk."

He smirked, a lazy smile that promised me dirty things if only I asked for them. "It'll go faster if you take over."

I crossed my arms beneath my breasts and glared at him—not because I hated the idea, mind you, but because I was pissed at myself for being so tempted. "I'm not helping you rub one out."

"Why not? Might make you feel better." He closed his eyes and groaned while rolling his palm over the crown, then sliding back to the base. "I helped you. Remember? You came all over my hand."

My nipples were so hard they ached. "You seem to be doing just fine without me."

Those dark blue irises locked with mine, and hunger burned within them. "I was. But now that you're here and not just in my mind, things are different."

"You were thinking of me while stroking your cock?" The breathless quality of my voice gave me away; I was sure of it.

"Sparrow, it's always you." He took his bottom lip between his teeth and let out a ragged breath as he picked up the pace. "Every." Stroke. "Single." Stroke. "Time."

My thighs quaked from being squeezed together so hard. I wanted to pretend I was unaffected. That he hadn't just obliterated the wall I was desperately trying to keep between us.

Fuck.

"Cross," I whispered.

"If you're too afraid to touch me, at least give me something."

I bristled at the obvious challenge, but I wasn't going to fall into his trap either. I was not getting in there with him. No way in hell.

"I don't want to touch you. There's a difference." I slipped the T-shirt over my head, baring my breasts to him and cupping the full weight of one in my palm. "But no one said I didn't want to touch myself."

"Christ," he grunted, squeezing himself at the base, eyes locked on my fingers as they teased my nipple.

"What's wrong, Cross? You never seen a pair of tits before?"

His lips pressed into a tight line. "You know I have. Yours happen to be my favorite."

"Oh, so you wish it was you doing this, then? God, it feels good, especially when I tug on my nipples while I roll my clit with my other hand."

"Fuck, sparrow. Keep talking."

I was playing with fire. I knew it. But I didn't care. Part of me welcomed the burn.

I slid my other hand down, dipping beneath the waistband of my leggings and finding myself already slick and swollen. I didn't admit all of this was for him, not to myself and not to the man about to come all over his own hand.

"What does it feel like?" he breathed. "Is your pussy as hot and wet as I made it the other day?"

"Wetter."

"Why?"

"Because I'm doing it myself. I know how to get the job done."

A muscle twitched in his jaw. Oh, he didn't like that.

"I know what you like."

I hummed, my eyes fluttering closed as I applied the perfect amount of pressure. "Maybe. But I know what I love."

"Dammit, sparrow."

"Bet I can make myself come before you do."

"Get over here, and I'll get us both off."

"No thanks."

Hand shuttling across his length, he breathed heavily and kept his hot stare on my tits. Knowing he was watching and reacting to me made a simple act into something far more erotic. I was lightheaded from my desire, panting as my climax came racing toward the finish line. His cock swelled even further, the head glistening with precum and his abs tensing over and over.

"Fuck, sparrow. I'm gonna come. Wanna come on your perfect fucking tits."

I shook my head, but secretly, that was a fantasy I'd entertained before. "Say my name when you do."

"River," he grunted, and a pained moan escaped him as his cock throbbed and ropes of his release spurted onto the tile.

I had to lean back on the counter as my own orgasm rocked me, my knees going weak from the blinding pleasure.

The water cut off while I was still coming down from my high. Cross's expression reminded me of a lazy, sated lion as he reached for a gray towel and wrapped it around his hips. "I won."

"What?" I asked, brain foggy from my orgasm.

"The bet. I came first."

I snorted. "Are you ready for your prize?"

"Give me five minutes and I will be."

Tugging on my shirt, I retreated as he began a slow stalk toward me. "Not so fast, stallion. I'm not the prize."

"You are from where I'm standing."

I hated that my stupid heart flipped at that. Traitor.

"Walker is."

That got his attention. He blinked. "Wait, what?"

"Congrats, champ. You're on Walker duty. I need a shower of my own."

I turned on my heels and gave myself a mental pat on the back for not letting him see how shaky I still was as I headed out of his room.

"The detachable shower head has ten different settings, sparrow!" he called after me. "You can thank me later."

Not about to have him get the last word, I paused and glanced over my shoulder. "Oh, I know. Number five is a personal favorite."

Then I winked and got the fuck out of there before I did something stupid. Like sit on his face.

fourteen

. . .

Bishop

SIREN:

What are you doing right now?

ME:

Who wants to know?

SIREN:

Cross.

ME:

Don't tease.

SIREN:

I miss you. It feels like it's been forever. Where have you been?

ME:

It's been two days.

SIREN:

Like I said. Forever.

ME:

I'm working on something for Cross. I should be back soon.

SIREN:

Does it have to do with . . . you know.

ME:

I can't answer that.

SIREN:

I don't like not being able to see you. I worry when you're gone.

ME:

I'll take that as a compliment and not a question of my skills. I'll be fine, baby. I promise.

She didn't know just how much it meant to me that she cared about my safety. I smiled and ran a hand over my beard, sighing through the fatigue of a long stakeout. I'd been living in this truck, surviving on protein bars and bottled water.

My fingers hovered over the illuminated screen, ready to send another message, but a call came through.

I hit answer and barked out, "Yeah?"

"Is that any way to greet an old friend, Bishop?"

"You're hardly my friend."

Deputy Assistant Director Douglas Wilson was my handler and a giant pain in my ass, definitely not someone I'd consider a friend. But in my line of work, he was as close as I had.

"I'll take you off my Christmas card list, then."

"What do you want? I'm busy."

"We need an update on your assignment. The higher-ups are getting restless. It was supposed to be a long game, but the Russians have been making big moves. The timeline needs to shift too."

Unease soured in my belly. "Things have changed since Senior's death."

"I know that."

"She's thrown a huge wrench in the plan. She's innocent and can't get hurt in the crossfire. Not without drawing a hell of a lot of attention from the media."

"I saw the announcement. She married him, huh? That's a development no one was expecting. It doesn't change the fact that the Cross family is going down."

"It wasn't like that. Her dad and Senior did it without them knowing. Told them both they were business documents, then filed the paperwork without their knowledge. They've been legally married for the last ten years."

"Jesus. That's cold."

"Yeah, well. It offers her a little more protection."

"Does it? Seems to me it only makes her a bigger target. Volkov will see her as leverage now."

Nausea rolled in my belly. Instinct had been whispering the same to me, but I'd been trying hard to ignore it. Especially while I was so far away and unable to keep an eye on her.

"He already did. He's smart enough to know he just has to get his hooks into her, one way or another."

"All the more reason for us to wrap this up. Get us what we need so we can put these guys behind bars. She'll be safer if they're all out of her life."

"Yeah. Maybe."

"You don't agree?"

I scratched at my chin, my eyes still trained on the warehouse across the street. It was close to midnight, and any legitimate work had long since ceased. "It's starting to feel like the Cross brothers aren't as involved in things as we suspected."

Wilson snorted in derision. "Yeah, and I'm the fucking cookie monster. Whose name is on those trucks? Whose pockets are lined in cash from dirty shipments?"

He was missing the point. "I'm serious, Wilson. They're involved, no question, but they're not the big bad here."

"Bishop. Have you been compromised?" His tone was suddenly all serious. Icy. Deadly.

"No. But our focus should be on—"

"Our focus is on whatever the hell I tell you it's on. Now get me what I need to put Daniel Cross Jr. in prison for the rest of his natural life."

Swallowing back an insubordinate reply, I bit out, "Any word on her parents?"

"You're living under the same roof as the people responsible for their deaths. But you already knew that, didn't you?"

"Did one of them pull the trigger?"

"May as well have."

"That's not the same—" A shadow moving in my periphery had me shutting my mouth mid-sentence. "Gotta go."

I hung up on Wilson and snagged my binoculars, adjusting the focus to see if my shadow was of the human variety. It was.

"What are you up to, you shady motherfucker?" I followed him until he stopped near a building, hoping I could figure out who he was now that he'd stepped into the beam of the floodlight. Unfortunately, he was so backlit all I could make out was his cowboy hat. If I was going to get eyes on him, I'd have to change positions or get out of my truck, but that would leave me exposed at best and blow my cover at worst.

"Come on, show me your face, asshole."

I reached for the camera I'd left on the passenger seat without taking my eyes off the unknown cowboy. As I watched, a trio of figures came into view. I had no trouble clocking those three, and they weren't trying to hide themselves either. Volkov's men didn't live in fear of discovery. They did their dirty business where anyone could see them because they thought they were untouchable.

Snapping a few pictures, I grinned as I caught them shaking the cowboy's hand. "Gotcha."

As the man in the middle pulled his hand away, I realized they hadn't been shaking hands. They'd been exchanging money. The cowboy seemed to count it and made to pocket it, but I was able to snap a couple more pictures of the exchange before he gestured for them to follow him inside.

"Goddammit, move out of that fucking light. I need to see your face, you traitor."

The words gave me pause. I shouldn't care about who was double-crossing the brothers, but I'd been on this assignment long enough I supposed it was only natural to feel a little bit of loyalty.

Yeah. Right.

Fucking idiot.

Falling in love with the one woman I couldn't have and forgetting where my true allegiance belonged. This was like something out of the handbook of cautionary tales for newbies.

I cursed as the group walked away. Whoever he was, the cowboy was smart. He stuck to the shadows and never gave me an opportunity to catch his face. I couldn't decide whether that was due to dumb luck or years of practice.

Either way, one thing was sure.

Snagging my phone, I hit the call button. Cross answered on the second ring.

"What?"

"You've got a big fucking problem."

"Yeah? Tell me something I don't know, asshole." Cross sighed, and I could picture him squeezing the bridge of his nose. "What now?"

"I know how the Russians are getting their info."

"How?"

"You've got a mole."

fifteen

. . .

Cross

Staring out over the lush green pasture in front of the lodge, I let Bishop's words wash over me for the millionth time. I'd been up all night trying to figure out who it could be.

A snake in the grass at Twisted Cross Ranch was the last thing I'd expected.

Call me naïve, but these people were more than ranch hands. They were family. Most of them had been with us for years. Hell, Tex took over after his father died. It wasn't just the family business for us. It was true for most of them as well.

No one at the ranch would betray us. Would they?

They sure as shit wouldn't have if Senior was still alive. But he's not. Which put the blame squarely on my shoulders.

Three cowboys rode by on their way from one pasture to another. One gave me a wave, and I simply raised my coffee cup from my place on the front porch in response. Was he the traitor? Jesus, I was getting paranoid. But all my life, I'd known I would be the one who kept this place going. I'd been trained to take on my daddy's mantle. And fuck, I wanted it.

Now, though? I seemed to be flushing everything my family had worked for, stolen, bled, and died to have, right down the drain. All I'd ever known was that I'd be his successor.

And I was failing.

No wonder he had River in his back pocket.

I couldn't help but wonder how'd he know she'd do a better job than me when she'd been sent away and had absolutely no idea what the job entailed. Had he been keeping tabs on her? Seemed like the kind of thing he would do.

Maybe that's why it stung so bad. He knew she'd go into this blind, and still he made the call.

The weight of the last few weeks was crushing me. Between her return, my father's death, the multiple attacks on my brother's life, and now this . . . I was losing my goddamn mind. Nothing was making any fucking sense.

"You won't get yourself any answers by sitting on your ass and whining about it," I muttered to myself.

Trouble was, I didn't know where to start. Without a name, I couldn't exactly *do* anything. And going after Dominik without a fleshed-out plan was a suicide mission. The only thing in my life I could actually work on right now was my relationship with River. And even that was a damn minefield.

She was guarded when it came to me, with good fucking reason. I'd done plenty of damage, especially after she came back. But the other night in my shower was a start. That was the most playful she'd been with me. Hell, it was the most conversation the two of us had shared without her nearly slapping me. If I'd had it my way, I would've torn those little leggings off her and fucked her against the shower wall until she forgot anyone else existed.

She made me crazy.

The worst part was she knew exactly what she could do to me.

Maybe I should text her. I let that tempting thought roll through my mind.

She was probably with Walker, tending to him and being sugar sweet. I never got that side of her, except for the first time we'd been together. Now it was fire and sass. If I was being honest, I fucking loved how she made me work for every inch with her. It was going to make winning her over that much sweeter. I wanted it all, though. Every single piece of her.

Too bad that would never happen. She'd already made it damn clear that parts of her belonged to someone else. Multiple someones.

"Speak of the devil," I muttered, sipping my coffee as Bishop drove up the drive.

He got out of the truck and slammed the door, his eyes ringed with dark circles. I would have felt bad, but I was paying him handsomely to do the job.

"Cross," he growled. "You're looking bright-eyed and bushy-tailed this morning."

"And you look like death."

"Feel like it too," he said, walking up to join me. "Next time, you can be the one living in the cab of his Ford. I'll stay here in the mansion with the pretty girl."

I wondered if he knew she'd made herself come for me. If he was as jealous as I'd been when I'd found her on her knees for him.

"You do remember that the pretty girl is my wife, right?"

"Yup. You're welcome, by the way."

"For what?"

He snorted. "Didn't you wonder why she was suddenly so amiable about being shackled to you? Why she didn't end up filing those divorce papers? I'm the one who told her to stay married to you. So I repeat, you're welcome."

I narrowed my eyes at him. "Why would you do that? What's in it for you?"

A slight shrug lifted his shoulders. "Her."

"How is being my wife going to get her for you?"

"I'd much rather she stay alive. And once she's out of danger and ready, she'll leave you and come to me."

Over my dead body.

I didn't say that though, instead I just raised a brow. "You think so, huh?"

"I know so."

"Don't count your chickens, Bishop."

I took a long drink of my coffee, even though it had gone cold, and pretended his words hadn't rattled me. There were a lot of ways our future could play out, but in every scenario I'd entertained, she ended up with me. A wife in more than name. A wife who loved me and wanted to be here. The one who'd been stolen from me by circumstances we couldn't control. Because I had no doubt if things had been different ten years ago, that's what she'd be now.

And I wouldn't have had to share her either.

I didn't realize I'd growled into my coffee cup until Bishop snickered.

"Fuck off. You smell like shit."

"Wow. Going for the low-hanging fruit, huh? We work with horses and cattle. Everyone on this ranch smells like shit. Daily."

"Yeah, well, you're offending my delicate sensibilities."

He laughed, and for some reason it made me hate him a little less. "What's the saying? All hat no cattle? I understand it so much better now."

Hearing him use my father's favorite expression—even if it was to take a jab—made me grin. This back and forth felt familiar. A little slice of normal amidst the chaos. I couldn't help but welcome it.

"Just because I don't get out there like I used to doesn't mean I can't ride circles around you, Bishop."

"Is that a challenge?"

"Name the day and time."

Bishop's lips twisted up in amusement, his teeth flashing. It might have been the first time I'd ever seen him smile. That was a weird thing to notice, but up until recently, our interactions had been pretty limited, and he'd always been a surly motherfucker. I guess watching my wife suck his dick changed things—even more than him saving my brother's life had.

Fuck. We were going to have to be friends, weren't we?

I was about to lob another challenge his way, this one involving who could get River off the hardest, when the rumble of an engine caught my ear.

Bishop tensed beside me. "You expecting company?"

"Nope."

We both reached for our weapons. His in a shoulder holster at his side. Mine at my hip. Neither of us drew right away, but both of us were ready.

The Harley Fat Boy didn't look custom, but the man rolling up on it seemed right at home. He came right for us, coming to a stop almost directly in front of the steps leading to the front door. Cutting the engine, he stood, removed his helmet, and then turned to look at us.

The man was easily six five, maybe taller, with a burly beard and dark hair pulled back in a messy bun at the base of his skull. It would look feminine on anyone else. On him, it just added to his intensity. His leather jacket and dark jeans didn't do a thing to hide the muscle on him either.

"Not another fucking step, friend. Unless you want bullet holes decorating that jacket of yours," I said, drawing my gun and taking aim.

"Is this what they refer to as southern hospitality?" The deep rumble of his voice was low and confident. Not a trace of tension or fear could be found in the question. It told me a whole helluva lot about him. The man had stared down the business end of a barrel before. More than once, if I had to guess.

"We don't take kindly to strangers appearing on our doorstep uninvited."

"Who says I wasn't invited?"

He took a step toward us, and I cocked my gun.

"That's close enough."

"Jonah!"

River's excited exclamation caught me off guard.

"You made it!"

She flew through the front door and would have continued down the steps if Bishop hadn't caught her by the wrist and pulled her back.

"What the fuck do you think you're doing, siren? You do not go running in front of a loaded gun."

She glanced between Bishop and me, her happy expression darkening. "Put the fucking gun away, you psycho. This is my friend, Bear."

I'd do no such thing. "I don't care who he is, sparrow. How the fuck am I supposed to run this place with unannounced visitors showing up all the damn time?"

"I told you he was coming."

"You absolutely did not. Because I can tell you for certain, I would've said no."

Her scowl deepened. So much for whatever ground I'd thought I'd won in the shower.

"You don't run this place anymore, remember? This is my house. Which means I can invite whoever the fuck I want to come over. Now put. The gun. Down."

Bear chuckled, and I really wished I had a reason to shoot him. Maybe just in the kneecap so I didn't kill him. But I holstered my piece and let out a begrudging sigh.

Bishop let go of her, satisfied that she wasn't about to walk in front of a bullet, and she resumed her flight, throwing her arms around the beast of a man. He picked her up easily, her legs wrapping around his waist with a familiarity that had my fingers itching to return to my gun.

I turned my head toward Bishop, dropping my voice so only he could hear. "Who'd she say that guy was?"

His arms were crossed over his chest, expression unreadable. "That's Jonah Blake. Goes by Bear. He's the one who saved her life when she moved to Alaska."

Guilt flashed through my system. Why had she needed saving? What had happened to her after I made sure she got sent away?

"He in love with her?"

"Who isn't?" Bishop said on a laugh. "But no. He's like a brother. A big, protective, dangerous brother."

"She doesn't need more protection. We've got her taken care of."

Bishop shook his head. "Clearly she doesn't see it like that."

My brows lowered. "You saying she thinks she needs protection from us?"

His lips quirked, and he shook his head. "Not us. *You*."

Sonofabitch.

sixteen

. . .

River

Ten years earlier

My stomach audibly growled as I made my way inside Hemlock Harbor's only bar and grill. This little Alaskan town was supposed to be my fresh start. Instead it had become one never-ending nightmare. First with the bus ride from hell with all manner of people from unwashed and predatory individuals to college kids trying to get home. I was ninety percent sure the woman next to me was offering her services to the other passengers and about seventy percent sure the driver was her pimp.

Then I arrived on what was supposed to be my grandmother's doorstep, only to find a public auction notice posted on her door. She'd died about two weeks before I'd arrived, and none of us had known. The thought made me ache. What if the same thing happened to me? I could die in this alley, and none of the people I loved would ever be the wiser.

And if that shit sandwich wasn't enough, I'd gotten myself mugged. My money, my ID, my laptop, my clothes . . . all gone. My body was one giant bruise, and I could only just hide the goose egg on my temple by creatively styling my greasy hair over it. I'd also rewashed my jeans and long-sleeve T-shirt so many times in the park bathroom that I was starting to get holes in them. I didn't know what I'd do when the weather turned. Die, I guess? I didn't even have a jacket. They'd find me frozen on a park bench and call me a Jane Doe.

As I walked inside the bar, I was hit with the scent of fries and hops. Not my favorite, but it was warm. Even this time of year, Alaska was colder than I was used to. A woman with sun-damaged cheeks and stringy dishwater blond hair eyed me up and down as I approached.

"What do you want? You don't look old enough to be in here."

I glanced around. "It's a restaurant, right? I'm eighteen. You don't have to be twenty-one to be in a restaurant. I need a job."

She frowned. "We're not hiring."

"There's a help wanted sign in the window."

Rolling her eyes, she turned her head away from me and hollered, "Hank! Your customer!"

A towering man with ebony skin and a shiny bald head came out of the back. His face was kind, which I appreciated after the shit I'd been dealt the last few weeks. I was really sick of people kicking me when I was down.

"What can I do for you, young lady?"

"She wants a job," the woman offered as I opened my mouth.

"I think she can answer for herself, Linda."

"Uh, yeah. It's like she said. Your sign out there says y'all are hiring."

Hank looked me up and down. "You ever worked in a restaurant before?"

"No, sir," I said, my manners kicking in.

"You're not from around here, are you . . ." The way he let the question hang told me he was waiting for my name.

"River."

He nodded, waiting for the rest of my answer.

"What gave me away?" I asked, trying for a smile but ending up with something more along the lines of a grimace. My face still hurt from being slammed into a brick wall, but at least the bruising had mostly faded.

"I'm originally from Oklahoma myself. I recognize a bit of southern drawl when I hear it."

"I really need a job, sir. I'm desperate for something. Anything. I'll wash dishes, take out the trash. Clean your bathrooms."

"You got any ID?"

I tried to hide it, but my lower lip wobbled. "N-no, sir."

"You're not a runaway, are you, River?"

Technically, that's exactly what I was. I'd run as hard and far away from Cross as I could manage. "My parents know I'm here."

He crossed thick arms over his chest. "And they sent you out here with nothing? That doesn't seem right."

"I was mugged in the park. They took everything I had."

He sighed as he looked me over, taking in my bedraggled appearance. "I can't hire you with no ID. You could be a minor for all I know."

"I understand. Thank you for talking to me." As I turned to leave, my stomach growled again, and he caught me by the wrist.

"Hang on. I might not be able to give you a job, but I sure as hell can make sure you eat something."

"I d-don't have any money."

"I understand that. You don't need it today. Now, go sit in that booth over there, River. I'll be back with a hot meal for you."

My legs all but gave out on me when I slid onto the forest green vinyl bench. My whole body was trembling with the aftereffects of too much adrenaline. This was the first time I'd felt safe since leaving home. And it was temporary. I couldn't exactly move in and live beneath the Formica table. Though it was a tempting thought.

My eyes watered as the reality of my situation crashed down on me, but I shoved the tears away. They wouldn't do me any good. I'd eat, and I'd figure the rest out after.

Hank slid a plate in front of me minutes later. It was a big juicy burger and fries, something I normally wouldn't have ordered for myself, but today, it might as well have been a steak.

"Thank you," I murmured as the scent of the food made my belly clench in anticipation. I was ashamed to say I'd spent days picking through the trash just to feed myself something. I'd had enough moldy bread and cold, half-eaten pizza to last me the rest of my life. It was a good day if I found an apple or any other piece of fruit.

"I'll be right back with some water and a milkshake for you. Strawberry okay?"

Oh God. A milkshake. I'd kill for a milkshake. I nodded when I realized he was waiting for my answer.

Why was this man being so nice to me? After everything with Cross, after the rush to send me away, and what I'd dealt with since showing up in town, I didn't know if I could trust anyone.

It made me sad that I'd lost that last bit of naivety. Growing up on the ranch, I'd never had to worry about things like that. I knew I was loved and would be taken care of. Alaska had been a cold dose of reality in more ways than one.

I tried to be polite for about ten seconds as I daintily dipped a few fries in my container of ketchup, but as soon as they hit my lips, the floodgates were opened. I went from hungry to ravenous, attacking the meal with all the fervor of a starving dog.

The door opened as I was stuffing my face, and I barely registered the giant of a man who entered. All I could think about was getting this food in my mouth before someone took it from me.

The giant walked over to Hank, and I couldn't help but notice that the dark ink tattooed on Hank's forearm was also on a patch decorating the giant's black vest. I'd watched enough episodes of Sons of Anarchy to recognize what I was seeing. They were in a motorcycle club. But the question was, were they the good kind of bikers or the organized crime kind? That was the last thing I wanted to get wrapped up in.

Don't be so high and mighty. Men who don't care about the law might be more inclined to overlook your lack of ID and offer you a job. You can't afford the moral high ground right now.

Hank approached and slid the milkshake across the table to me. He'd even added sprinkles and a cherry to the top.

"You need another burger, kid?" he asked, glancing at my nearly empty plate.

"I'm not a kid," I growled around a mouthful of burger. "And yes, please. If you don't mind."

The giant hovering right behind him laughed. "Yeah, Harley, she's not a kid. She's a fierce little cub. She growls and everything."

I looked between them with a frown. "I thought your name was Hank?"

"It is. But my brothers call me Harley."

"You two don't look like brothers," I commented after chasing my half-eaten fries with a gulp of ice cream.

"Family can be built in all sorts of ways, cub. You can call me Bear." He held out a huge palm, his fingers stained with grease I recognized from when my dad would work on our car. Maybe he was a mechanic?

Or a biker, you silly goose.

"River. Nice to meet you," I said, using my arm to wipe away something greasy from my chin.

Bear smirked as he slid into the seat across from me, and I simply allowed it. I was too hungry to care if I had to share a table with him.

"Harley tells me you need a place to stay."

"Harley sure is chatty."

"It's pretty obvious you've been living on the street, cub. He said you got mugged?"

I nodded, taking another long drink.

"I've got a place not far from here. How about I set you up with some work and a place to stay?"

Little alarm bells went off in my mind. There was only one reason a man would offer a girl a place to stay for free. I was desperate, but I wasn't that desperate.

"No thanks."

His brows flew up. "What?"

"I'm not going to go shack up with some old dude I just met."

He started laughing. Great big guffaws that made his eyes crinkle at the corners. He didn't look so scary when he was smiling. "Damn, girl. You know how to cut a guy, don't you? I'm not *that* old."

"Old enough for a beard," I grumbled, eyeing the thick, bushy length that did nothing to disguise his cheekbones. He was probably around Cross's age, but he looked a little rougher around the edges, with his big muscles and tattoos. Everything about him was a threat, and yet I still felt safe. Safe enough to poke at him. "Plenty of men your age are just lying in wait for girls like me to turn eighteen."

Cross's blue gaze flashed in my memory. But that wasn't what had happened between us. No matter how much he'd hurt me, he wasn't the kind of creep who chased the barely legals around town. I knew better than that. If anything, it was the other way around. They chased him. Myself included.

Unaware of my internal self-flagellation, Bear chuckled and stole one of my fries.

"You're a smart girl, cub. You misunderstood me, though. It's not just me you'd be staying with. I live with my sister Virginia. Gigi," he clarified. "She's about your age and is sick of being stuck with just her grumpy older brother for company. I figured you two could keep each other out of trouble."

"So you're getting her a puppy to be her friend."

"No. I'm helping you out and making her happy. It's a win-win."

"You can't just bring me home with you. I'm not a stray."

"Sure you are, cub. Nothing wrong with that. We've all been there at least once. Don't be so stubborn you refuse a lifeline when it's offered."

I chewed on that for a minute. Walker always told me I was too hardheaded for my own good. Maybe he was right.

"Okay. But if there's any funny business, I won't hesitate to castrate you. I used to spend a lot of time on a cattle ranch, and I've seen a bull made into a steer."

He grimaced, then let out a low chuckle. "I think you and I are going to be fast friends, little cub."

"I have a name, you know."

"Yeah. Cub."

I shook my head, but there was no hiding my smile. It was the first real smile I'd had since arriving here. The weight that had been sitting heavy on my shoulders and chest fell away, and it felt like I took my first easy breath.

Things were going to be okay.

I was going to be okay.

Present day

AS SOON AS Bishop released me, I bolted toward Bear, pure elation at seeing him again flooding my veins. I leaped into his arms and hugged him tight, my legs wrapping around his waist as I clung to him like the lifeline he'd been the last decade.

"Good to see you, cub," he murmured, soft enough the other two men who were watching couldn't hear.

"You too. You were supposed to call me when you landed. I would have picked you up at the airport."

He laughed. "You know how I feel about riding in cages."

I shook my head, biting back a laugh at the MC's familiar euphemism for any vehicle that wasn't a motorcycle. "Where did you get the Harley?"

"Buddy of mine has a shop down here. He loaned her to me."

"Her, huh? This lady got a name?"

"Precious."

I snickered. "Obviously. How did I not know that?"

"Are these two gonna give you grief about being all over me like this? They're giving me murder eyes."

"I don't care. They don't own me."

"Do *they* know that?"

"If they've been listening to what I say, then yes. I can hold on to you however long I need to." Even so, I got down and released him. It was just so good to have my friend here. I hadn't really been gone that long, but it felt like a lifetime.

Jonah and Gigi had been my only family for so long. I hadn't realized how homesick I was for them until I caught the familiar smell of home on him.

My expression must have reflected my shift in mood, because Bear tipped my chin up. "Hey, now. What's goin' on, cub?"

"Nothing," I said, forcing a smile. "Just missed you is all. You up for a tour?"

"After a few introductions. Which one of these big swinging dicks is the husband?"

I laughed, gaze flicking to Cross as I pointed. "That one."

"You can call me Cross." My husband stepped forward but didn't offer a hand to shake.

"You do anything else to hurt her, I'll call you a dead man."

Jesus.

"We don't take kindly to threats around here, Mr. Blake." Cross's eyes were shaded by the brim of his hat, but I could feel them boring a hole into me. "I take care of what's mine. River included."

"Apparently you aren't doing as good a job as you think since she called me."

Cross's lips peeled back in a snarl, and I was pretty sure he was ready to launch himself at Bear, but Bishop caught him by the back of the shirt, keeping him in place.

"You hurt him, she won't forgive you," Bishop said in a soft warning.

"It can be one more thing she adds to the list," he muttered.

"There's a list?" Bear asked.

"A fucking mile long," I said with a sigh.

"And who is this guy? Do we like him?" Bear's focus was trained on Bishop, suspicion in his eyes.

I softened as I followed his gaze, my lips tipping up as I took in my sexy giant. "We do. We like him a lot."

Cross bristled but didn't say a damn thing.

Bishop grunted and tipped his chin up. "Name's Bishop. Nice to meet you."

Despite my affirmation, Bear didn't seem too impressed with him. "Why'd you call me if you have him?"

It was probably the politest way Bear knew how to ask him how he fucked up and let me down.

"It's complicated. But you're here now, and I'm so glad."

Cross looked ready to murder me, which twisted up feelings inside me that I wasn't prepared to deal with.

Hooking my arm through Bear's, I forced my attention away from the two men in front of us and looked up at him. "Come on. Let's see the house I inherited, then maybe we can go for a ride."

Bear made a face. "I'm not getting my fat ass up on one of those toothpick-legged fuckers."

"Don't talk like that about my friend. But also, these horses are strong. They can carry you, no problem."

"I'll stick to my steel horse. You can ride your pony alongside me. How's that?"

"No way in hell—" Cross started, but I interrupted him.

"I'll do what I want. And first, I want to show Bear *my* house."

We walked past Cross and Bishop, and thankfully neither of them stopped us. But as soon as we were on the path to the house, Cross offered one parting shot.

"Be sure to introduce him to your other boyfriend."

I stiffened as Bear dropped his gaze to me. "One husband wasn't enough? You have multiple boyfriends too?"

Heaving a sigh, I squeezed his bicep and rested my head on his beefy shoulder. "It's a long story."

"Good thing my schedule's wide open. Start talking, cub. And don't leave anything out."

"Why did I invite you out here again, bossy britches?"

He laughed at the old nickname. "Because you love me."

"Shit. You're right, I do. Well, in that case, it was a dark and stormy night . . ."

seventeen

. . .

Walker

I fucking did it. I was heaving for breath, sweating profusely, and thought I might die, but I fucking got out of bed and into my wheelchair by myself. It wasn't a graceful maneuver by any stretch of the imagination. With one bum leg and second-degree burns on my feet, standing was basically impossible. So it was more of a calculated fall into the chair. I was just lucky the fucker had brakes, otherwise I might be stuck doing my turtle impersonation on the floor until the next time someone showed up. I was sure my brother would've loved to see me fail.

Take that, Cross. I can *do things on my own.*

Was it fair I was blaming him for my current predicament? Probably not. Was it easier than blaming myself? Abso-fucking-lutely.

According to my doctor, my chair days were still a ways off, but I needed to get out of this room, away from the bed that had been my prison for the last week. Fuck, I needed fresh air and sunshine and . . . River. I wasn't gonna get any of that if I didn't stop feeling sorry for myself.

"Okay, partner, let's get this show on the road," I said to my new ride. "Hi ho, Silver . . ."

The door opened as I raised my arm gingerly—because my ribs still smarted and my body was still in rough shape—and pretended to slap the chair on its hindquarters.

River let out a surprised giggle while the hulking stranger behind her raised his brows.

"Uh . . . I can explain."

"How medicated are you?"

"Juuuust enough." I jutted my chin at the man accompanying her. "Who the hell is this guy? Did y'all spring for a bulky nurse to replace you as my sexy one? Or have I started hallucinating?"

River's lips twitched before she smiled and took the asshole's hand. What. The. Fuck? Was she collecting us?

I groaned. "Don't tell me there's another one. I just came around to the idea of sharing you with Bishop and Cross. I can't make room for this guy."

Her nose crinkled in disgust. "This is Bear. He's one of my closest friends, and *no,* we are *not* sleeping together."

My shoulders relaxed a little at that. "I was one of your closest friends . . ." I let that hang for a minute.

"Me fucking Bear would be like you fucking Cross."

I shuddered. "Got it."

Bear's low, rumbled laugh got my back up all over again. "Listen, if you were in love with her, you'd understand."

"Oh, I do. She's special to me. Like my little sister. Which means I'll be watching all of you for any reason to kick your ass."

"Do I really look like a threat?" I gestured to my new wheels. "My ass has been thoroughly kicked, I assure you."

"You deserve it?" he asked, surprising me.

"Depends on whose side you're on."

"River's. Always."

"Then no, definitely not."

"You get any hits in?"

"Kinda hard to defend my honor when I'm outnumbered and three sheets to the wind."

"Ah, it was like that," Bear said, nodding. I wasn't sure if it was in understanding or some bizarre sort of approval, but he looked like the kind of guy that had seen his share of barroom brawls. "A little sloppy, don't you think?"

"Drowning your sorrows always is."

River's eyes were cast down when I glanced over at her. Guilt was etched on her face. I hadn't given her that information because I was the idiot who let my guard down. I hadn't wanted her to know I'd been drinking because she'd hurt me.

"Hey, ladybug, look at me," I murmured. "It's not your fault I was stupid."

"Yeah, but—"

"Nah, no buts." I gave her a lascivious wink. "Unless it's yours in my lap."

She closed the distance between us, leaned down, and feathered her lips over mine, whispering, "As soon as you can handle it, I'll take you up on that."

My dick liked the way she was talking. A fucking lot. Too bad I couldn't do a damn thing to help him out. "Give me a few more days, darlin'."

"Aren't you being a little optimistic?" she teased as she straightened.

"Nah. I've always been competitive. Soon as someone tells me I can't do something, I have to prove them wrong. And you just gave me a heavy dose of motivation."

She shook her head. "You're going to end up hurting yourself worse."

"Then you'll just have to kiss me better."

Bear cleared his throat. Right. We had company.

"So, what do you two have planned today? Any chance it's a jailbreak?"

Backing away, she rested one hand on her hip and gave me a dubious glance. "Stairs."

I gestured at the giant mountain man she had at her side. "Andre the Giant."

"Did I volunteer for something without realizing it?" he asked.

"You were voluntold." I batted my eyelashes. "You afraid of getting too close, big guy?"

He scoffed. "I'm afraid of hurting you and making River mad."

River sighed and stared at me. "Most guys wouldn't be okay asking another man to carry him down the stairs like he was a damsel."

"You say damsel, I say king."

"How do you figure?" she asked.

"Remember those dudes who had to carry the kings around on pillows and shit? That's me. I'm the king. They're the ones doing all the hard work."

"You're really selling this to me," Bear said, sarcasm dripping from every word.

"You're sleeping under my roof."

"River's."

Damn.

"Touché. Look, I'm secure enough in my masculinity to ask for help when I need it."

"Tell that to your brother," River shot back. "He had to force you to let him help."

"That's different. He's a dick."

"The dickiest," River agreed, making Bear and me laugh.

"I thought you liked his dick?"

River's mouth dropped open at Bear's dig. "What the hell gave you that idea?"

"I'm new here, not fuckin blind. I saw the way you two looked at each other. You can lie to yourself, cub, but you never could lie to me."

Her cheeks blazed crimson, but she didn't back down. "You don't have a say about whose dick I like, so the point is moot. Wouldn't you agree? Or do you want me weighing in on how often you like to get yours wet with what's-her-tits who works at the corner store?"

I watched their bickering with a wide smile. I'd always known she was amazing, but this was fucking special. The only times she went after people like this was if she felt safe with them. It made me look at Bear with new appreciation. He was one of us. Well, not *us* as in the us that wanted to dick River down. But family.

I was glad she'd had him in her corner when I couldn't be. She deserved that kind of loyalty and unconditional love.

"I'm not getting any younger here," I said, holding my arms up.

"You can wheel your damn self to the stairs. I'm not carrying you any longer than I have to." Bear turned on his heels and headed out.

River raised her brows in challenge when I didn't follow him. "Well, what are you waiting for?"

"Ladies first."

Her eyes narrowed. "You just want to stare at my ass."

"Duh."

She gave her hips a little extra sway as she walked, and I knew it was for my benefit. Carefully wheeling myself out of the room and down the hall, I thanked my lucky stars this house had been built with space in mind. Getting around would've been nearly impossible if the halls and doorways weren't so big.

"And on your left, you'll see yet another dead ancestor," I intoned.

Bear gave the walls a cursory once over. "What is it with rich people trying to create their own fucking museums? Do you even care about these dead white dudes?"

"Nope. Some of them have real nice hats, though."

"I'm partial to old Robert there and his walrus mustache," River offered.

"He was the black sheep of the family. No one liked the 'stache."

"Really?"

I laughed. "How the fuck should I know? If I could, I'd take down every one of these portraits and burn them."

"Even the one in your dad's old office?"

"That one would go first," I said with a snort. "Pretentious old fuck." We reached the top of the stairs, and I glanced up at Bear. "How are we doing this? Bridal or fireman?"

His brows lifted into his hairline. "What?"

"You know, the carrying. Are you tossing me over your shoulder like a sack of potatoes or cradling me gently?"

"Jesus fucking Christ," he muttered, glaring at River. "I am never visiting you again. First I'm held at gunpoint, and not an hour later I'm schlepping around this asshole. You owe me."

"At least I always pay my debts."

I lifted my arms and made grabby hands. "Come on, Daddy. Pick me up and take me for a ride."

"Now I know you're high," River said with a giggle.

"Oh fuck yeah. There was never any doubt."

She leaned into Bear, one hand on his forearm. "Don't you dare put him over your shoulder. He's got broken ribs."

"There's only one way he's going down these stairs, cub, and that ain't it. Come on, you rodeo clown."

Bear carefully picked me up, and I'm not ashamed to admit I whimpered and had to bite back a cry of agony when my leg began throbbing through the haze of pain meds. But before long, we were on the ground floor, River was opening up my chair, and the sunshine was within reach.

"Ah, tastes like victory," I crowed, even though I was still coated in sweat from the aftershocks of pain. Guess the doc might have been onto something when he said it was too soon for the chair.

We went through the house together, me playing loopy tour guide, them laughing at my antics. Once we reached the back porch and settled in the sun, I let myself relax. I closed my eyes and soaked up the sound of her happy conversation with Bear, the chirping of birds, the whinnies of the horses in the distance. I'd missed this. Being laid up wasn't something I was used to. I fought through injury and illness every time. But this one . . . this had nearly killed me, so I didn't have much of a choice.

Cracking my eyes open, I slid my focus to the pool, the water still as glass. "And here, you can see the swimming pool where River became a woman."

"What? No! I did not lose my virginity here."

"Did I say that? I meant the time you got your period in front of me and Cross when you were twelve. All over that white towel you were laying out on."

"Don't make me dump you in the pool," she threatened.

"You love me too much."

"These things are not mutually exclusive," she said mulishly, crossing her arms and leaning back in her chair.

Bear laughed. "Consider it your repayment for my efforts."

"Hearing embarrassing stories about me?"

"Fuck yeah."

Sitting up a little straighter, I smirked. "How about the time I caught her with her hand—"

She threw a pillow at my head in an attempt to shut me up.

She missed.

I kept right on talking.

She'd make me pay for it later, but if that meant I got alone time with her tonight, then the joke was on her. I couldn't fucking wait.

eighteen

. . .

Cross

I rapped my knuckles on Walker's door, doing a final check before heading to bed. When there was no immediate answer, I cracked it open and looked inside, finding him splayed out on his bed with River curled into his side.

My brother may have always thought I got everything he wanted, but as I stood in the doorway of his room, I realized he couldn't have been more wrong. He had her in his arms. He had her heart. And me? All I had was a fiery connection built on anger and hurt. She might let me make her come on my fingers, but she would never willingly sleep beside me through the night. That little bit of vulnerability was reserved for the man—men?—she trusted.

"Fuck, sparrow," I said under my breath as I raked a hand through my hair. "What's it gonna take to make you love me again?"

River stirred in Walker's bed, her soft sigh of my name hitting me straight in the chest. I doubted she knew all the ways she had me tied up in knots. I had been ever since the night I'd broken us.

But then her sweet voice took me down at the knees. "I never stopped loving you. 'S why it hurts so bad."

Suddenly, I couldn't stand the thought of her spending the night beside him. She was my wife. She belonged with me. Her brows furrowed, and a little pout turned down her lips as she shifted to her side.

Crossing the room, I reached for her, hesitant for a beat before shaking her awake.

"Come on, baby, let's go."

"Mmm, I'm comfy." Her voice was thick with sleep. Calm. Relaxed. Everything she wasn't when I was around.

"I can see that, but you can't sleep here."

"Why not?" she asked, her words slightly slurred as I scooped her up into my arms. "Walk asked me to stay."

"I'm sure he did," I grumbled. Thankfully, I had a logical, if not downright inspired, excuse why that was a terrible idea. "But you could hurt him without meaning to, and he would never tell you about it."

River frowned, eyes still closed, head resting on my chest. Goddamn, she smelled good. "I don't want to hurt . . . you."

I knew this was the haze of sleep talking, but it was also an opening for me to share my truth. I could crack the cold and hard veneer I've been hiding behind, if only right now. "It's me that did the hurting. Let me make it up to you."

She nuzzled into my warmth. "Mkay. I'm tired of fighting . . . even if you're hot when you're mad."

A low chuckle rumbled from my chest. "You rile me up like no other."

"Even Cici?"

Where did that come from?

"Like I said. *No* other."

A little smile curled her lips. "Good. You're mine."

My eyebrows flew up at that shocking confession. If I'd known she'd be this chatty and honest in her sleep, I would have paid her a nighttime visit weeks ago. I didn't even have it in me to feel guilty about uncovering truths she never meant for my ears. This was fucking ammunition, and I sure as hell was going to use it to my advantage.

Dropping a kiss to her temple, I inhaled her sweet scent one more time before I kicked open my bedroom door. Should I have taken her to her own bed? Yes. Was I going to? Fuck no.

Especially not after she claimed me like that.

She snuggled into me a little deeper before I pulled back the blankets and slipped her under the covers.

"Mmm. Smells like you," she murmured, but then opened her eyes, finally coming fully awake. "Wait. This isn't my bed, Cross."

"Nope, but it's where you belong, *wife*."

She started to sit up but froze, her vision clearing with every heartbeat. And there was no mistaking the hunger in those pretty green irises as she studied me, weighing her options. Wanting to sway the vote in my favor and not afraid to play a little dirty, I didn't say a word as I unbuttoned my shirt, then tugged it off. Her eyes devoured every inch of skin I had to display. There was a lot more where that came from.

"If you really don't want to be here, you can go. But I've been desperate to feel you next to me for ten fucking years, sparrow, and I'm not above begging you. If you're gonna share anyone's bed tonight, it should be mine." I unfastened my belt, confidence shaken because I knew she should reject me. "Please?"

Sitting up, she pulled back the covers next to her to welcome me. But what really got me was the look in her eyes as she tore the flimsy, too-big T-shirt over her head.

"Jesus, fuck," I whispered at the sight of those perfect full tits. If I hadn't already been hard as stone, I would've been at full mast in an instant.

Careful not to rush, I shoved my jeans down my hips, thankful as hell we didn't wear our boots in the house.

"Commando, huh?"

"Wranglers don't leave much room. Especially not with how I wear 'em."

She smirked, eyes on my dick. "They sure don't."

"Lie back for me, beautiful. I want to look at every part of you until I can see you with my eyes closed."

She opened her mouth like she was going to argue. Hell, I was expecting her to. It had become our thing. But she didn't say anything, just made a little humming sound and obeyed.

"Do you like it when I take charge in the bedroom? That's unexpected."

"Why's that?"

"You fucking hate it everywhere else."

Her back arched like a cat searching for more affection as I ran my palm between her breasts and down her belly.

"Maybe I have to be so in control of the rest of my life, I want a break from it in bed. Maybe I just want you to take care of me and make me feel good, Cross."

"Take off your panties. Now."

A hitched breath was her only response before she did what I told her.

"Hand them to me."

Again, she did. I brought the scrap of lace to my nose and inhaled her sweet scent before tossing the garment on top of my pile of clothes. She wouldn't be getting those back.

"Cross," she whispered, her voice breathy with need.

"I've got you, baby. If you let me, I'll make you feel so damn good you won't remember your own name." Her eyelids fluttered as my fingers trailed across the neatly trimmed thatch of hair between her legs. "Is this pussy wet for me? When I open your thighs, will I find you glistening and ready for me to suck your needy little clit until you scream?"

"Maybe you should stop talking and go find out for yourself."

I smirked, recognizing her bluff. She was trash for my dirty mouth. She just didn't want to admit it. But the way her nipples were a deep red and pulled tight into desperate points proved me right.

I moved away from her, loving the small sound of protest she made before I knelt on the bottom of the bed, taking an ankle in each hand so I could slowly spread her open. Just as I suspected, she was soaked. I crawled up between her legs, my hands gliding along the silky skin of her thighs. I never raised my gaze from my goal, so I caught the flood of arousal as it fell from her. My fingers dug into her soft flesh as I pushed her legs further apart.

"Tell me how much you want me."

"Haven't you ever heard of show, don't tell?" she teased.

"I'm an auditory learner, sweetness. I need to hear it."

She sucked in a tight gasp as I framed her cunt with my hands, not touching her where she truly wanted it, but promising I would.

"I've always wanted you, Cross. Even when I hated you. I'd wake up in the middle of the night with my fingers in my pussy and your name on my lips."

I rocked my hips into the mattress so I could get a little friction on my throbbing dick. She had me strung tight. Needing her as on edge as me, I blew a focused stream of air across her fluttering cunt.

She squirmed and moaned, an attempt to escape and a plea for me to put her out of her misery all at once. But I held her fast, not letting her get away. I was going to eat her until she came on my face, and then I'd fuck her until we both passed out.

A panicked thought raced through my mind. I didn't have protection. Not here. I never brought women home. This was my sacred space, not a fuck pad. I'd have to put on the brakes, and that was the last thing I wanted to do with this goddess under me.

But a spark of something else ignited in my head, the forbidden thought making precum leak from my aching cock. I could make her mine in every way with nothing between us. Maybe I'd even knock her up. Tie her to me for the rest of our lives.

Fuck, I wanted that. To fill her full of my cum and make her thick with my child. To breed her.

Her fingers threaded in my hair, tugging my face up so I had to stare into her eyes. "Stop teasing me. Please."

"Tell me what you want, baby."

"Everything you want to give me."

She wouldn't have dared to say that if she knew the direction my thoughts had taken. Still, I couldn't help but smirk at her. "Careful what you wish for. I'll give you the moon if you fucking ask me to. But right now, I want to give you the ride of your life."

"Better get to work, cowboy."

She positioned my face right over her slick cunt, and I groaned as I parted her lips with my fingers. "My pleasure, ma'am."

nineteen

• • •

River

Daniel Cross Jr. had a way with his tongue that rivaled almost anything I'd ever experienced. He turned going down on a woman into a fucking art form. I'd never be able to watch him lick a spoon again without spontaneously combusting. His stubbled cheeks brushed my inner thighs as I clamped them around his head, the rough scrape only adding to the eroticism of this moment. That, combined with the feel of my fingers buried in the soft strands of his hair while I shamelessly ground my pelvis against his face, had me chanting his name.

He lifted his head, eyes rolling up to meet mine. "You taste like everything I was missing, sweetness."

"And you're better at this than I remember."

The vibration of his low, rumbled laugh along my slick folds made me moan. "I knew you'd never forget me."

"Shut up and make me come, Cross. I'm dying."

Part of me thought he'd drag it out and tease me, but he seemed just as eager to make me climax on his tongue. Instead of responding with words, he spread me open wider and sank two fingers inside me, his focus on my eyes the whole time. All I got from him was an intense stare and a little smirk when I squirmed. Then he dove back in, licking and sucking my clit until my thighs trembled and I was reduced to a whimpering mess.

"That's it, baby, ride my face."

I bucked against him like an unbroken filly, which only made him double down. His fingers beckoned inside me, thrumming against my G-spot while he used his other hand to press down on my lower belly and increase the pressure.

The man hadn't been exaggerating when he said he'd get me the moon. This orgasm was sure to launch me up into the stars.

"Fuck, Cross. I'm coming."

"Come for me, wife," he rumbled against my clit. "Right fucking now."

Back bowing, I rode out my release with my hands tangled in his hair and my hips pinned to the bed. I hoped the other two men in my life realized I was safe here with Cross. Otherwise we were about to have company because of the screams I let out. Fuck, maybe Bishop still would. Or Bear. Jesus, the last thing I needed was my quasi big brother finding me with my legs spread and dripping pussy on display.

Cross sat back, breathing heavily, lips and chin glistening with my arousal. "That's my good girl. You come so pretty."

I couldn't speak. I was too lost in the hazy edges of the euphoria he'd given me. Instead I opened my legs wider and waited for him to give me everything I wanted. He hadn't been inside me in a decade, but my body still craved him the same way, possibly more.

He'd already proven to be better than I remembered. It was time to find out if his dick had leveled up as much as his tongue had.

"That smile for me, sparrow?"

I wanted to tease him. Tell him I'd been thinking about Bishop just to try and restore some of my control, but I didn't have it in me. The truth was, I'd been here with him a hundred percent of the way. And I wasn't close to being done yet.

"Maybe."

His eyes went hard, and that smile on his face disappeared, replaced by determination. "We'll have to do something to make sure the answer is yes."

"Then what are you waiting for?"

He positioned himself over me, his hands on either side of my head as he brought his lips to mine. I could taste myself on him and understood why he liked it so much. A possessive thrill ran through me knowing he smelled like my cum. I wanted him to wear it everywhere he went.

The tip of his dick slid through my seam until he was all but notched at my entrance. I gripped his hips and rocked mine, eager to help him sink home, but he stiffened and held himself back.

"I don't have a condom," he murmured, forehead resting against mine.

"Don't care. I'm on the pill. Have at it."

A feral growl vibrated in his chest at the permission. "Are you sure? That isn't one hundred percent effective. I could still knock you up, sparrow. Then you'd be mine forever."

"Isn't that what you really want, anyway? To claim me as yours?" His dick twitched against my opening. Oh, he liked that idea. "Do you want to fill me up? Does the idea of me having your baby get you hard, Cross?"

I wriggled, and he sank in the barest inch, pulling a ragged groan from him.

"You know, I'm not sure if I took my pill this morning. It's been so crazy around here. I may have forgotten."

"Fuck, sparrow," he grunted, thrusting into me before I could keep egging him on.

My broody and dangerous cowboy had a breeding kink. I was sort of here for it.

The feel of him inside me, stretching me wide, was everything I'd dreamed about during those long Alaskan nights. It felt like coming home. Tears pricked my eyes, and I had to blink them away. Just because I decided to give him my body didn't mean I had to give him my heart.

Not yet, anyway. The fucker could grovel a while longer.

But doesn't he already have it? Hasn't he always? My traitorous inner voice reminded me of the truth, and I didn't want to listen.

"Look at you, taking my dick like such a good fucking girl, sparrow. God. I could live here and never want anything else. You are so fucking perfect. Made for me. Made to take my cock."

Oh, he was a talker now. I liked that a whole hell of a lot, especially when he told me how much he wanted me.

"Keep talking," I rasped.

His lips twitched as he continued his slow, rolling thrusts. His mouth might be pure filth, but there was no doubt that Cross was making love to me with his body. The combination of the two, the worship mixed with the sexy words, was making my brain short-circuit.

"I'm gonna imprint myself on you from the inside out. You won't be able to take a step tomorrow without feeling the memory of me buried deep. Fuck, baby, your pussy squeezes me so tight. If I was a weaker man, I'd have come inside you already."

"God, Cross. I can't . . . it's so good."

Rocking his hips again, he filled me all the way to the hilt and stopped there, staring at me. One palm skated across my collarbone before he wrapped his fingers around my throat and held himself there. He didn't apply pressure or tighten his hold on me. Cross simply collared me as he resumed that hypnotic roll of his hips, his pelvis applying the perfect amount of friction to my clit with each pass.

"You're close, aren't you?" he whispered, his voice tight as he clearly worked to contain his own approaching climax. "Do you want me to fuck you full of my baby, River? Tie you to me forever? If I don't pull out, that's what's gonna happen. You'll never be rid of me then. No matter how hard you try to convince yourself you're better off without me." His fingers flexed on my throat, his eyes burning mine with the intensity of his stare. "You're mine, sweetness. You always have been."

It was all I could do to bite out, "Yes." I didn't know what part of his speech I was responding to. All of it? Maybe.

I was lost to my pleasure, to my heart finally getting a decade-old wish. Cross with me, wanting me, choosing me. It didn't erase the past, but fuck if it didn't ease the sting.

"Cross, I—"

"Come for me. Milk my cock, baby. Show me how good it feels when I love you."

Jesus, I was done for.

I detonated around him, my vision going black at the edges as I came with a ragged cry of his name. Finally, he sped up his pace, the sound of our flesh slapping together joining his heavy breaths. I thought he'd been trying to come with me, to weave his orgasm into mine, but instead of filling me full like he promised, he pulled out at the last moment. Taking himself in his fist, it only took one rushed stroke before he painted my chest and belly with hot spurts of his cum.

The way his abs contracted as he found his release was mesmerizing. Those defined ridges rolling along with the involuntary jerking of his hips were as captivating as the sounds he made. Cross had always been a beautiful bastard, but watching him fall apart for me . . . because of me, was everything. If this man hadn't stolen my heart ten years ago, I would have given it to him then and there. Not because he was an amazing lover, which he absolutely was. God, he was. But because in that moment, with his blue eyes burning with emotion, there was no hiding how he felt about me.

"River . . . I . . ." He dropped his gaze to my belly, staring at the evidence of what we'd just shared.

"I thought you had better aim than that, Cross. How're you gonna get the job done like this?"

God help me, his dick began thickening where it lay against my lower belly. "We're not ready for that yet, sweetness. You may have been forced to be my wife, but I'm not gonna force you to have my baby until you're safe."

"So you *are* going to force me to?" I teased with a raised brow.

"We both know when the time comes, you're going to be begging me to knock you up, sugar."

"Someone's feeling sure of himself."

"Someone just heard the way you screamed his name while your cunt gripped his cock like a vise. So yeah, I'm feeling pretty damn good, sparrow."

I bit down on my bottom lip, feeling reckless and needy. "Put it inside me, Cross. That's the only place your cum should be."

His eyes flashed with hunger, and he trailed one finger through the mess he'd made. "You sure? It's risky."

"I like to live on the wild side."

He growled in response before scooping his release into his hand and slipping his cum covered fingers inside me. It was hard to tell which one of us enjoyed it more. There was no denying the look of satisfaction stamped across his face as he stared down at my pussy.

"You're mine now, baby."

My belly gave a happy swoop, even as a little voice in the back of my mind admitted the truth.

I always have been.

twenty

. . .

Bishop

All I wanted to do was check in on River before bed, but with Bear visiting and Walker insisting he was ready for his wheelchair, I knew she had her hands full. I could wait a few more days.

So instead I'd headed to my room and planned to settle in with my laptop and some work. Wilson had sent me some encrypted files I hadn't gotten a chance to check out. I was hoping whatever he'd found might be the key to solving the riddle of River's parents' deaths. Or if not that, perhaps it would point me in the direction of whoever was sending her those packages.

As soon as I opened the computer, though, every plan I'd had went out the window. A notification flashed on my screen, making excitement burn in my belly.

VOICES DETECTED: CROSS JR. BEDROOM

While I had research for River to do, I also had my own assignment, and hopefully the bug I'd planted in Cross's bedroom would finally give me something I needed. I checked the recordings once a week before archiving them, but this was a live feed, meaning whatever I was about to hear was happening right now.

His voice came over the speaker as soon as I clicked the play button. *"That's my good girl. You come so pretty."*

"Fucking asshole. Who do you have in there with y—"

"That smile for me, sparrow?" he continued after her breathy moans and sighs subsided.

Sparrow. So he'd finally gotten River under him.

I'd expected a pang of disappointment or maybe jealousy, but both emotions were oddly lacking. If I was jealous, it was only because I wasn't in there with them. I kept listening, desperate to hear her arousal-soaked voice. My dick was already hard and straining behind my sweats, a wet spot visible on the front of the fabric. Jesus, the things this woman did to me with nothing but her sighs.She really was a siren.

"Maybe."

Her voice had me shoving the computer off my lap and reaching into my pants without a second thought.

"We'll have to do something to make sure the answer is yes." Cross sounded as hungry for her as I was. I understood exactly how he felt.

"Then what are you waiting for?"

"Motherfucker," I hissed, pushing my pants down around my thighs and stroking my throbbing length slowly, a bead of precum collecting on the tip.

I could picture her splayed out on the bed, hair fanned across the pillow like a golden halo. If she was with me, she'd be kneeling in front of me. Bound with silk rope, knees wide apart and held in place by the ties connecting her wrists to her ankles. Christ, she'd look beautiful like that. At my mercy. Her pleasure mine to command.

"Fuck," I groaned alongside Cross and River as they both made needy sounds.

"Fuck, sparrow. Look at you, taking my dick like such a good fucking girl."

She was *my* good girl. He was just lucky to get her first. I'd make up for it as soon as I could.

My phone rang on the bedside table, an insistent vibration I wasn't interested in seeing to. Not now. Not when I had River's moans to keep me company.

With each rustle of fabric or whimper from her, I fell deeper into my fantasy. One with me in place of Cross. Or maybe her between us again.

My siren would beg for us to touch her all over, and we would, but we'd tease her first. I'd bite her ripe nipples until they were red and swollen while Cross sucked her clit until she was nothing but a quivering plaything for the two of us. Pliant, warm, wet, and open. And only when she was trembling and praying for release would I shove Cross aside and sink my fat cock inside her. He's had her before. He could feed her his dick or come all over those tits for all I cared. As long as I was the one buried to the hilt this time.

"God, Cross. I can't . . . it's so good."

"You're close, aren't you?"

I needed her to come so I could. My hand shuttled along my cock, faster than I wanted, but I couldn't miss her orgasm. I may not be the one inside her, but I wanted mine to happen with hers. Reaching between my legs, I grabbed my balls and held tight, the pain usually a solid way to keep me from coming too soon. But I was too far gone. Especially once her breaths came in sharp gasps.

"Yes. Cross, I—"

"Come for me. Milk my cock, baby. Show me how good it feels when I love you."

I groaned as her strangled cry of pleasure filled my room, and I erupted along with her, my release splashing over my hand and belly. I hadn't made a mess like this in years. My siren had turned me into a fucking teenager.

I vaguely heard Cross murmur something as I came back to my senses, but I slammed the laptop closed, wishing I could be the one with her right now.

You could be. All you have to do is go in there and stake your claim.

The temptation to do just that was real. My cock was stirring again at the thought of joining them for the next round, of being the one making her cry out.

He owes you after you shared her with him earlier. She'd let you stay. She'd want you to.

I hadn't been so driven by desire for a woman in . . . maybe ever.

All I needed was her. All I fucking craved was her.

She'd ruin me if I let her.

Let her? Buddy, you'd fucking beg for it.

I grabbed a tissue off the side table and tried to clean myself up, but it was no use. Just the thought of her, combined with her needy moans, had made me come like a fountain. I gave up and headed to the bathroom. Pulling off my clothes and tossing them in the hamper, I turned on the shower and washed off the remnants of what River did to me.

That sorted, I wrapped a towel around my hips and went back to my computer, intent on actually getting my work done. But once again, my good intentions were thwarted. My phone was going off like a damn vibrator.

Grumbling, I snatched it from the table and stared down at the seven missed calls.

"Jesus, Wilson. What could be happening this late that you can't wait until sunup?"

But I knew in my gut what this meant. Something big had happened. And I'd ignored it.

"Bishop," I barked, a less than friendly greeting, but at this point, we were in a no-nonsense situation.

"What the fuck is going on with you? You answer when I call, Agent Bishop. Every. Fucking. Time."

"What part of undercover do you not understand? I am not always going to be at your beck and call, Wilson. Not without risking my mission."

The assistant deputy director grunted. He couldn't deny the truth of my words, even if rubbing one out didn't exactly fall under the umbrella of 'covert ops'.

"Your mission objective is shifting. At least for the time being."

"What?" That was a huge breach of protocol. Undercover agents didn't just get reassigned on the fly.

"Girls are going missing within a hundred-mile radius of Twisted Cross Ranch, Agent Bishop. And you are in a unique position to do something about it. We send anybody else in now, we risk not only blowing your cover but tipping our perps off. It has to be you."

"Missing? How many?"

"Fifteen so far have disappeared in the last two weeks. No trace of them to be found."

"Ages?"

"Between sixteen to thirty-five. All pretty loners, with small families or just a few close friends or work colleagues."

"Someone to miss them but not enough to draw serious attention."

"Exactly. And they just vanish off the street. Like they never existed."

My gut churned. He could've been describing River. "And there's nothing to indicate they're already dead?"

"Hard to say without the bodies or even a crime scene."

"So we aren't thinking this is a serial?"

"No. Not yet, anyway. Intel says that the Russians look good for it."

My stomach sank. "You think they're getting ready to sell them."

It wasn't a question. Volkov was known for this very thing, but we hadn't had a way into his exclusive auctions so we could make arrests. And I happened to know for a fact he was in the area. He couldn't keep that many girls hidden for long. This was happening soon. Weeks if we were lucky, days if we weren't.

"What do you need me to do?"

"Keep your ear to the ground for any rumblings about an auction, a gala, a meeting at the fucking Russian bathhouse."

"What about Cross?"

"Until you hear otherwise, Agent Bishop, consider this your sole priority. You and I both know what will happen to those girls if we don't find them first."

A chill raced down my spine. I'd seen this before, but we found them too late with no way to tie their sales to anyone aside from the men who'd bought them. Most of them were dead by the time we tracked them down. Used up and thrown away like broken dolls. Not this time.

"Is Cross involved in this?" I asked, thinking of the woman I wanted so badly being wrapped in his arms right now.

"We have no evidence to suggest he is."

I relaxed a little at that.

"But we don't have anything suggesting he isn't either."

Fuck.

twenty-one

. . .

Walker

"Lucky bastard doesn't realize how good he's got it right now."

Cross let out an affirming grunt, his eyes locked on River and Bear as they stood outside the stables. Two horses were saddled, Bear giving his a dubious look. He wasn't gonna tell her no, but I could see it plain as day—that man didn't want to ride.

They were too far away for us to make out their conversation, but I could easily see the giant's lips move as his scowl deepened. River's answering giggle floated to me, and a slight frown worked its way between my brows. I'd woken up this morning expecting to find her in my bed, but she'd been long gone. If not for the faint scent of her perfume on my sheets, I would have doubted she'd been there at all.

What was it about this guy that relaxed her so easily? With us, she was like a cat in the bath. With him, she was curled up in a beam of sunshine, purring happily.

Cross looked just as twisted up about their relationship as I was. He'd joined me on the porch this morning, an ease in his posture I hadn't noticed in a long time. Then the second River and Bear came into view, he'd tensed up again.

It was on the tip of my tongue to ask what was going on with him when I got my answer in the form of his expression.

Hunger.

It was right there, blazing in his eyes as he watched her.

"You asshole."

He turned his face toward mine. "What did I do now?"

"You had sex last night. That's why she wasn't in bed with me this morning."

Bringing his mug of coffee to his lips, he offered a slight shrug before taking a sip.

"Taking advantage of her in a weak moment is not something I ever expected from you. She doesn't deserve that."

The look he gave me would have pinned me to the spot if I wasn't already sitting. "I didn't. She asked me to be with her. It wasn't just . . ."

"Fucking?" I finished after he trailed off.

"Right. It was more. *She* is more than that."

I scoffed, years of our old fights flooding my mind. "Of fucking course you'd decide you want her now."

"What the hell is that supposed to mean?"

"I think it's pretty obvious. You couldn't get far enough away from her until you found her with me. Then out of the fucking blue you finally decide you're interested. Finding out you were married just gave you a convenient excuse, but we both know the truth. You only want her because I do."

"Fuck you. That couldn't be further from the truth. If anything, it's the opposite. You've always wanted everything I had."

If I could've stood, I would've. I wanted nothing more than to get right in his face. "Can't you just let me have this one thing? I've loved her longer than you, and honestly, I spent too long being the good brother who respected her boundaries. I sat by and watched her fall for you, all the while craving her for myself. And you are such a fucking dick. You just hurt her over and over."

"You have no goddamn idea what you're talking about."

"Oh? Explain it to me, then. Tell me how you suddenly love her more than I do when, up until a week ago, you couldn't stand to be in the same room as her."

My brother's expression twisted, pain making his eyes so dark they were almost black. "You think you've loved her longer? Maybe you have, but only because I was too old for her so I never let myself think about her that way. Until I did. Until I fell so damn hard so fast my entire world flipped upside down in a single night. She was going to be it for me. She *is* it for me. I had our entire future mapped out, down to the fucking dog we'd have."

My stomach churned at the tortured cast of his voice. I'd never seen Cross so passionate about anything. Not even our father's death. I barely recognized him.

"So what happened?"

"Senior. Senior fucking happened. Decisions he made . . ." Cross trailed off, blowing out a heavy breath and shaking his head. "Let's just say he made it clear this was no life for her. She's too good for the likes of us."

"If that's true, why did he trick you two into marriage? That makes no goddamn sense."

His jaw clenched, eyes trained on the two figures slowly riding away from us. He swallowed hard. "Things can change as quickly as the strike of a match, little brother. You know that as well as I do. Once I saw the truth, I had to break her. She had to leave, get as far away from us as she could. I'd rather give up any chance of ever being happy than be the reason the light left her eyes. So I hurt her. I gave her no reason to stay. And I'd do it again if I thought it would keep her safe. I'd do anything if it meant I didn't have to watch her fall out of love with me piece by piece as the picture of what this family really is came into focus."

"What changed? If all that's true, why are you finally letting yourself keep her this time?" I hated the question as it left my lips, but a big part of me understood him all too well.

"I'm a selfish prick. I love her, but not enough to lose her again."

I wanted to call bullshit, but I recognized that look. I'd worn it often enough myself. The asshole did love her. Fuck. This changed everything. If he really loved her, that meant I was the asshole standing in the way of her happiness.

But I'd stood aside once, and it nearly killed me. In this, I was just like my brother. I couldn't be selfless and lose her again. I loved River too much to let her go.

"I'm not giving her up," I said.

"Me either."

"I know," I said on a sigh, resolved but not defeated. I could feel Cross's curious stare boring into the side of my face.

"So you're just gonna date my wife? The press'll have a field day with that."

"Frankly, I don't give a single fuck what the press thinks. The only person's opinion that matters is hers."

"So we leave the choice up to her?"

"You think you'll be able to handle it if she chooses me?" I asked, raising a brow as I glanced back over at him.

Cross's expression was unreadable as Bishop moved into our line of sight, heading toward the stable.

"What if she doesn't choose either of us?" he asked softly.

I couldn't bear to consider the possibility. "Or . . . what if she chooses all of us?"

The huff of laughter that escaped my brother was a mixture of incredulous and confused. "You think she would?"

"I'd rather that be the case than have to accept a life without her. I'm not too proud to share."

"You've never willingly shared anything a day in your life."

My brows lifted. "Maybe not with you."

Something in him changed as a flicker of interest raced across his face. "Is that something you've done before? More than one partner at the same time?"

"I've had a threesome once or twice. Nothing like what we're talking about, though."

"You really think we could do that? How would it even work? Long-term, I mean. She can't marry us all."

I shrugged. "I guess we'll have to figure it out. Because I'm willing to bet that guy is of the same mind as us, and if none of us are willing to give her up, the only other option is to make it work."

My brother chewed that over for a while. I could practically see the wheels turning in his mind. Eventually the silence became too much for me, and I blurted, "Well, what do you think? We gonna share our girl?"

"I'm not as opposed to it as I thought I'd be. We had a moment, me, Bishop, and River. It worked. In fact, it was fucking hot."

Holy shit. No fucking way.

"Without me? You guys suck."

He laughed, honest to God, a full laugh with no malice behind it. "It just happened. I came across them outside. She was sucking him off, and I . . . just joined them."

I shifted in my seat, my dick trying to tent my pants at the image of her on her knees between them. "I hate you all."

"If we worked together as a trio. I don't see why we couldn't add a fourth."

"Who are you?"

Cross's lips twitched. "Maybe you don't know me as well as you thought you did, Walk."

"Okay, well, we don't have to . . . do stuff to each other, right?"

He rolled his eyes and sighed. "That would be incest. I'm not getting anywhere near you. This is about our girl and giving her everything she could ever want. Not about getting anyone else off."

Yeah. I could work with that. In fact, I was looking forward to it. I loved the idea of her squirming with pleasure while she took everything we could give. River deserved the world. Who's to say it wouldn't take all three of us to ensure she got it.

"I mean, she does already have my last name," I said eventually.

Cross cuffed the back of my head. "*My* name, asshole."

"Maybe we should have a contest. First to put a baby in her wins?"

His self-satisfied chuckle told me everything I needed to know. "I've already got a head start on that, then."

"She's on the pill. You don't have a head start on a damn thing."

"Not for much longer."

"And you think you fucked her so good she'll just go along with that?" Part of me wanted to tell him how she'd called my dick magic, but I decided to keep that for myself.

He snorted. "What makes you think she hasn't already agreed?"

I shook my head. "Anything she agreed to post orgasm doesn't count. It's practically a law."

Cross grinned and shrugged, looking way too fucking smug. Something told me I would have to keep an eye on him. Fucker probably would toss out her birth control without her knowing. Replace them with sugar pills instead.

"We'll see. But before we can live happily ever after, we need to get Volkov handled."

I shuddered at the mention of the Russian mob boss who'd been instrumental in putting me in this chair. I wanted to be the one to put a bullet between his eyes.

"Agreed," I said, voice hard. "I don't want that piece of shit to get his hands anywhere near our girl."

"Our girl," Cross repeated, sounding almost reverent.

"So we're on the same page?" I asked. "We take out the trash, and then we see where this goes with her?"

"It's going all the fucking way, Walker. She's the one."

"I don't disagree. I just hope she feels the same."

He sat back in his chair, coffee to his lips again as he trained his gaze on River and Bear, who were slowly working together to get him up to speed on riding basics. Bishop was leaning against the outside of the stables, his attention on her as well. If the three of us worked together, we could get rid of the threat to our budding unit. But that meant we'd have to bring Bishop closer into the fold. He'd have to become family. One of us.

I was willing to bet that for her, he'd become anything she needed.

twenty-two

• • •

River

I giggled as Bear walked away, his usual smooth gait stilted. He had, as they say, a hitch in his giddy up.

"I hear you laughing, cub. I'm gonna make you pay for that later." He didn't turn around, but his voice was loud enough it carried on the wind. I only laughed harder.

God, I hadn't felt this light in a long time. Part of it was Bear being here, but another big reason was what happened last night with Cross. We seemed to have unlocked the gate separating us, and a sort of wobbly bridge had been constructed.

Butterflies fluttered in my belly every time I thought about our night together. It was almost like I was getting a re-do of our morning after. I didn't think we'd ever go back to who we'd been ten years ago, but this felt like a start in that direction.

I could still feel the soft feathering of his lips across my forehead as the sun came up and he started his day. Tender. Almost reverent. But it was his whispered words that did me in.

"I could get used to waking up beside you, baby."

It was the quiet yearning laced through them that made me think it was the start of something real. Maybe even forever.

A shiver ran down my spine at the memory. I inhaled deeply,

bringing the collar of the T-shirt I'd stolen from him up to my nose as I did. It smelled like Cross, made me wish I was still between his sheets, tangled up with him.

Hell, I needed to get a fucking grip. One night of passion in a cowboy's bed did not a forever make. Especially not this cowboy. He'd probably already shut down and gone back to the ice-cold facade he wore so well. Sex was great and all, but I'd be a fool to think it was magical.

Not ready to return to the house and face the rejection I was now convinced I'd receive, I roamed the grounds, heading for my favorite place on this ranch. The gazebo.

Imagine my surprise to find the cowboy in question already there, shoulders tense, hands gripping the railing as he stared out over the pond.

My steps faltered, and I debated leaving him in peace, but he must have heard me coming because he called out to me without ever turning his head.

"I never took you for a coward, sparrow."

I bristled in response, but there was so much warmth in his voice that the reaction was almost instantly washed away. Bolstering my own confidence, I joined him in the shade. "I'm not a coward. You just looked like you were doing some serious thinking. I didn't want to interrupt in case you were solving world hunger or something."

"Erectile dysfunction," he corrected.

His joke was so unexpected I had to swallow a laugh before offering a deadpan response. "Ah yes, the bane of every old man's existence."

He snorted, finally turning to face me. "I don't have a problem there. As you witnessed twice last night. And again this morning."

I blushed. "You're the one who brought it up. Figured you might be preparing for the future or something. You're turning fifty soon, right? I thought I spotted some salt in your pepper while you were taking a mid-morning nap."

"Ha ha. Very funny. Anyone ever tell you it's not nice to disrespect your elders?"

"I'll be sure to make a note. Although, I doubt you could read it without your glasses. Do you need me to make sure—"

He snagged my wrist and tugged me hard against his solid frame. "Shut up and come here."

Fingers threaded through the hair at the base of my skull as he pulled until my lips were on offer just for him.

"I've been dying to kiss you all damn day," he growled.

"Then what are you waiting for?"

His lips were on mine before I finished speaking. I melted into him, all my earlier fears evaporating beneath his talented tongue. My heart, which had been already protected by the thin walls I'd preemptively erected this morning, swelled and almost hurt from the relief his kiss gave me. Healthy? Nope. But I couldn't help it. Daniel Cross Jr. had me wrapped around his little finger and always would. That was the thing about addiction. Even when you know it's going to kill you, staying away is the hardest possible option.

I would always crave my next fix.

"Mmm, better," he rumbled, his eyes still closed when he pulled away and rested his forehead against mine. "Any chance I could convince you to let me lock you up in my room for the foreseeable future so we could do that on repeat?"

"Tempting, but I have a guest, remember? Pretty sure he'd break the door down to get to me. Not to mention your brother, who I'm helping nurse back to health."

"Don't forget your ranch hand. Something tells me Bishop wouldn't be okay with you disappearing on him either."

Heat blossomed in my chest. "Something tells me you're right."

"You're collecting us like studs to add to your stable, sparrow. What are you gonna do with us all?"

That sent a wave of lust through me in a way I wasn't prepared for. Well, except for Bear. He wasn't part of this equation, and Cross knew it.

"I don't know. I haven't really thought about it."

"Little liar," he teased, his voice a sexy whisper. "I bet you've thought about it a lot. Especially when you're taking those extra long showers."

"Does it bother you?" I asked, suddenly nervous again. Things were finally going so well between us; I didn't want to lose that just because my heart was a greedy bitch.

And by heart, do you mean pussy?

"That you want all of us?"

I nodded, biting down on my cheek to avoid blurting out an apology he didn't ask for.

He took my hand and pressed it against his already hard dick. "Does it feel like I mind?"

Swallowing through the lump in my throat, I murmured, "Not even a little."

"There ain't nothing little about what you do to me. And if you're as willing and wet as you were the other day with Bishop, I can't wait to do it again. But this time, when you're drinking him down, it'll be my cock inside you, not my fingers."

An unintelligible moan left me at the mental image. It was a miracle I was still standing with as weak as my knees felt.

"Maybe Walker will join us if he's feeling up for it. He told me once he really likes to watch."

The suggestion nearly had me coming on the spot. "You'd really be okay with that?"

"If it means I get to keep you, there's not much I wouldn't be okay with, sparrow." He took my chin between his thumb and forefinger, tilting my face so I was staring into his blue eyes. "I'm in, baby. All fucking in."

"Me too," I breathed, pinching my thigh to double-check that this was really happening and I wasn't in some lusty fantasy.

"I told you I'd get you the moon. I meant it. You're my wife, River. You can have it all."

I threaded my fingers behind his neck, asking him to hold me without words. He obliged, his arms going to my waist before his large palms settled on my ass. In the space between one kiss and the next, he lifted me until I was seated on the rail behind me and we were right back in the position we'd been in when we shared our first kiss.

"Tell me what you'll give me, Cross."

"Everything. All the things you wanted to have when you fantasized about your future."

"A family?"

His grin was all man. "I think I made that clear last night. But in case there was any doubt, fuck yes."

"Happiness?"

"Absolutely."

"Love?"

"More than you'll know what to do with."

Joy burst through me, only to be immediately chased away. Here I was, where I'd always wanted to be, and I couldn't allow myself to believe it was real. Confusion swirled inside my head, the events of ten years ago cracking the veneer of possibility he'd painted.

His eyes scanned my face, his smile slipping. "What is it? Where'd you go just now?"

"It's just . . ."

He nodded, urging me to finish my thought.

"I guess I just don't understand the change of heart after all this time. You could have had me ten years ago, but you chased me away. And then I came back, and you weren't exactly happy to see me. But now . . ."

The light left his eyes as he put a little space between us. "You left without a fight. You hated me for ten years. Why did *you* change your mind?"

It was a fair question, even if it was evasive. But if I expected him to give me the truth, I had to offer him the same. "Because I never really hated you. Even though I wanted to. Anger was my only defense."

Frustration burned through me. We'd already done this dance. We should be beyond it, but something niggled at the back of my mind, a little worm of doubt that I had the whole story. Because the man in front of me, the one who'd looked at me like he'd found his reason for breathing when he'd been inside me, could not have been the same asshole who so carelessly threw me away. Those feelings couldn't be faked, nor did they happen overnight, which meant there was more going on here. Pieces of the puzzle I didn't have.

"You could have come to find me. If you really wanted me, you would've stopped at nothing to get what you were after." My stupid voice wobbled. "You were, and still are, tenacious. Like a dog with a bone. Did I really not matter enough to you?"

He was shaking his head before I finished talking, eyes flashing with emotion. "You've got it backward, sparrow. You were the only thing that mattered."

"If that's how you treat someone important to you, no wonder you're still single."

"Except I'm not." He tucked a stray piece of hair behind my ear. "I don't know if you heard, but I'm a married man. And my wife is the most important thing in my world. Always has been."

I snorted, trying to hide the tears burning in my eyes. "Oh yeah? What about the note? You don't leave something like that for a woman if that's the case."

"You do when you're trying to protect her."

Sighing, I rested my palm against his chest, letting myself feel his heartbeat and the way his muscles tightened at my touch. "I need you to explain everything. If we're going to do this, you owe me the truth. I can't keep feeling so in the dark with you. I need for there to be no more secrets between us."

He glanced away from me, blowing out a breath. And for a second, I didn't think he was going to answer. I braced myself for the rejection, told my stupid heart we knew this was never going to last, but then he shocked me.

"You're right."

I backed away from him as much as my position would allow. "Go on."

"It's complicated. And a lot of it is ugly."

It was my turn to make him look at me. "I watched you shoot a guy, Cross. I don't exactly have illusions about the kind of life you lead. I'm not a delicate flower. I can take it."

Sadness flickered in his gaze before he replaced it with determination. "That's the thing. I wish you didn't have to. In my own fucked up way, I was trying to spare you from this."

"It's too late. Our fathers intertwined our fates a long time ago. I've been involved without even knowing it. And you can see how well that's gone. I have enemies I never even knew about. I can't live like this, Cross. I deserve to know."

Panic radiated from him as he sucked in a sharp breath. "You'll never look at me the same once you do."

"Let me be the judge of that. Tell me everything."

twenty-three

. . .

Cross

She didn't know what she was asking me for.

Everything meant so much more than simply laying my truth at her feet. It meant her whole world would come crashing down, and I'd be the instrument of her destruction for telling her. More than that, she'd lose her hero. I'd already taken so much from her; I didn't want to be responsible for that too.

But it didn't seem like I was going to get a choice.

"Where do you want me to start? It's not exactly a linear equation. There's no beginning, middle, or fuck, even an end to this story."

"Tell me why you left that note."

Anxiety had already turned my blood to ice. Tingles of apprehension were working their way up and down my arms. "I got a call that night. Several, actually. Which I missed because I was—"

"Deflowering me?" she offered.

"Yeah." I tried to smile, but I was too sick with worry to do more than grimace. A shuddering breath escaped me before I continued. If I was coming clean, she needed it all. "You need to understand, I was there with you, in awe of what I had, seeing our future plain as day. I was ready to marry you—"

"Apparently, we were already married."

"You know what I mean."

She nodded, her eyes bright with emotion. She was trying her best to make this easy on me, but there was no easy way. Not with a truth that would hit with the force of a fucking bomb.

Blowing out a breath, I continued, "But then I had to leave you there, sound asleep and so pretty it hurt to walk away. I met up with my father. There was an emergency he wanted me to check out with him and Casey."

"My dad was with you?"

I gave her a tight nod. "I didn't think much of it, you know? He'd been grooming me to take over for a while at that point, and I'd done similar things in the past. Following up on shipment issues or dealing with rascals stepping out of line. None of that prepared me for what we found that night."

"Cross, what happened? You're shaking. What did you see?"

"You're aware we're involved in more than our on-paper businesses. You're smart enough to have figured it out a long time ago. It's been going on for generations now, and Senior put us all in danger because of it."

"The second set of books," she murmured. It wasn't so much a question as her connecting the dots.

"Most of the illegal stuff goes through the shipping company. People pay us a lot of money for our connections. We know who can be bribed to look the other way, plus we offer the security necessary to transport certain types of goods."

"Drugs."

"And weapons. Sometimes other less obvious contraband."

"This is how you ended up in bed with the Russians," she guessed.

"Yeah, pretty much."

"Okay, I'm following. So what did you guys find that night?"

My stomach churned as flashes of dead bodies lined up on the ground raced to the forefront of my mind. "A fucking blood bath. We lost so much, so many innocent people. And the shipment . . . this time it wasn't drugs or weapons. It was women. My dad had sold his soul to the Russian mob, and we'd become traffickers without even realizing it."

She jerked as if I slapped her. "Your dad *knew*?"

"He swore up and down to Casey and me that he didn't. That if he'd known what they were using the trucks for, he never would have agreed, but the only one who knows for sure is him. He refused to tell either of us what happened to put him in a position to agree to any of their demands. Pretty sure that's a secret he took to his grave."

"My dad was involved in this? He was like you?"

God, she asked the last question with such disgust. Like me? A man who had blood on his hands. It hurt, but I'd earned it.

"Yeah. He taught me almost everything I know. My dad showed me the business. Yours showed me how to get the job done."

River looked like she was going to be sick.

"I know you don't want to hear this."

"Don't want to hear that the man who raised me wasn't remotely the person he pretended to be?" She laughed, but it was devoid of all humor. "I asked for the truth."

"And I gave it to you. He loved you more than anything. Once we learned about how far the Russians were willing to take things, the threats they made about you . . ."

"Me?"

"There were insinuations they'd do the same, or worse, to the people closest to us."

She blinked, her eyes cloudy with the weight of her thoughts. "So that's why you pushed me away. Why my father agreed so easily to let me go. Why he told me not to come back."

"We didn't want you anywhere near them. If something happened to you, I'd never forgive myself. I had nightmares for years about finding you in the back of one of our trucks. Dead. Because of me."

A little gasp escaped. "That's why I couldn't come back when my parents died."

"It wasn't safe."

"I understand why you thought you needed to do it. But it wasn't your decision to make. You chose to break me instead of trust me. You abandoned me. No, worse than that. You cut me off from *everyone* I loved."

"Sparrow—"

"I wasn't allowed to come to my parents' funeral. I wasn't able to say goodbye. I never got to tell my mother I loved her one last time. You took that away from me. All of you did." She raked her fingers through her hair, looking furious and devastated all at the same time. "My mother was tortured because your father got mine involved in this bullshit. I . . ." She started to hyperventilate, her breaths sawing in and out of her. "I need a minute."

She tried to jump down and push me away at the same time, her movement hurried and uncoordinated. In her rush to get away, she didn't realize I was trying to keep her from falling on her ass as my hands cupped her shoulders.

"Get the fuck off me, Cross."

"I'm just trying to—"

"You've done enough. Just let me go."

I'd known this was coming. That as soon as she learned the truth, she'd hate me on a level she'd never reached before, but it still gutted me. Panic sent the last of my sanity fleeing. I couldn't lose her. Not again. Then suddenly it wasn't just her furious with me, but me furious with her.

"No, goddammit. Just listen."

"No!"

"Everything I've done has been for you, you stubborn woman."

"That's rich. I'm sure Cecilia was definitely for me."

Ignoring the jab, I continued. "I never stopped fighting to keep you safe, not once. And even though I regretted not having you in my arms every fucking night, I knew it was better that you were alive."

"But you're just fine having me here now?"

"Of course I wasn't. I was fucking terrified when you showed up after all these years. I thought I knew what yearning was, but to have you in the same room and not be able to touch you. To know the precise way your cunt grips me, remember how you taste, and know I'll never get to experience either again. It was hell, and I was desperate to escape. But then I found out you were mine, and it was game over. It didn't matter what I'd fought so hard for all these years. I'd already lost. And won." I shook my head, feeling like I wasn't making any sense but desperate for her to understand.

"I can't do this," she whispered, voice tight with tears. "Let me go, Cross."

"I let you go once. Never again." She opened her mouth to protest, and I slammed my lips down over hers, kissing her with a passion bordering on obsession. "I know this was a lot to take in. I understand needing time to process it all. I'll let you take a walk and cool off, but I will be coming after you. There is nowhere on this earth you can go where I won't follow. You are my wife, sparrow. 'Til death do us part."

Pushing away from me, she closed her eyes, one tear trailing down her cheek. "Trust me to know what's best for me this time. You might be my husband, but you're not my keeper. And this corrupt claim you have over me means nothing if I don't choose you."

"Corrupt?" The word was jagged in my throat. She was breaking my heart with well-aimed shots.

"What else would you call it? I didn't knowingly agree to marry you. I was manipulated at every turn. Not just with the marriage, but what happened after. For once, can you please just let me choose for myself?"

It was on the tip of my tongue to say no, because what if that choice wasn't me? In the end, it didn't matter what I wanted to say because she was right. I'd had similar thoughts myself, fears that I would tarnish her. I guess I was a filthy corruptor. She'd said as much.

But we'd mended things between us, hadn't we? The way we came together in my bed, how right we felt together, how fucking much I needed her—all those things had told me she *was* choosing this.

"Last night—"

"Doesn't change anything." She shoved me with both palms on my chest, and I took one step back, giving her some room. Nudging me with her shoulder, she made for the house.

"River."

"Don't follow me, Cross. For once, please, just . . . leave me alone."

I watched her walk away, taking what was left of my heart with her.

She might think she'd gotten the final say, but she hadn't, not really. I'd give her the battle, but I'd be damned if I let her win the war.

Corruptor's claim or not, she was mine.

And I intended to keep her.

twenty-four

• • •

River

Leaving Cross alone in the gazebo hurt almost as much as learning my father was a monster. But I couldn't stand there and take in his words anymore, not without falling under his spell all over again and letting go of the biggest issue. My dad wasn't who I'd thought he was. He'd been my hero my whole life, but if Cross was anything to go by, Casey Adams had done terrible things.

My stomach churned as I realized those payments in his name suddenly made sense. He was being paid off for his part in Senior's criminal underground. And as close as those two were, my dad was no silent partner. His hands had to be as dirty as the rest of them.

I was going to be sick.

Had my mom known?

Was he the reason they'd been captured and tortured to death?

Was this the secret I'd been sent here to uncover? It had to be, but what was to be gained by me finding out? Or perhaps I should be asking who stood to gain by me finding out. Certainly not the Crosses. If anything, it only painted them in a negative light.

But worse than that, it raised an even bigger question. Was the Cross family the cause of my entire life falling apart?

When the answer came, it was accompanied by a wave of grief. Of course they were. They were at the center of it all. No matter which way you looked at it, it always came back to them. Their family. Their bad choices. Their enemies.

Daniel Cross Sr. and his handsome sons had ruined my life. Over. And over. And over again.

And I'd fucking let them.

I was such an idiot.

A burly arm caught me about the waist as Bear's voice rumbled in my ear. "Whoa there, cub. What's got you so wound up?"

I blinked up at him, the rickety walls I'd been erecting already crumbling under his attention. "I'm fine."

"You're not. Who hurt you?"

I badly wanted to blame Cross, but it wasn't his name I uttered.

"My dad," I whispered, voice wobbling.

Bear blinked, clearly not expecting the words. "Maybe you should back up and start at the beginning."

So I did. Leading Bear to the porch swing, I sat down and waited for him to join me. Then, for the next hour, I spilled my guts to the only man I had trusted in the last decade. I'm not ashamed to say I cried about all of it.

My burly bear wrapped me up in his arms, holding me tight. Every now and then, he'd whisper encouragement against the crown of my head, running surprisingly gentle fingers through my hair. I hadn't been held like that in years, like there was someone else in my corner ready to fight all my battles and take on the world in my honor.

"Come home, cub. You don't belong here."

Backing away, I looked at him, taking in the sincerity in his eyes. "What? I can't."

"Yeah, you sure as fuck can. You don't owe these jackholes a damn thing. Pack your shit. We can leave tonight."

Was that what I wanted? To run away and leave this mess behind?

Part of it was tempting, but a bigger part of me mourned the thought.

I didn't want to leave Sterling or Walker behind. I wasn't even sure I wanted to leave Cross behind, though it might be a while before I sought him out again.

"I . . . I don't know if that's a good idea."

"Trust me, cub. It's for the best. You belong at home with the people who love you."

But this was my home. It always had been.

Until it wasn't.

"It's not so simple. None of this is."

"Seems simple to me. You're miserable here. They can't give you what you need, and you deserve better."

"I'm married."

"So? Get divorced. Everyone else does."

"You're not listening to me."

"All I've done for the last hour is listen. I can't help it if you don't like that I see through the bullshit."

"I don't want to leave them."

"Who?"

Any of them.

But that didn't seem like a smart answer, considering all I'd just revealed.

"Walker is still healing. He needs me. And Bishop, he's helping me solve my parents' murder. I can't just abandon him after all the work he's put in doing this for me."

"Does it really matter who pulled the trigger? Will it change anything for you to have a name after all this time?"

"I don't know. But it might. Never knowing is worse."

Bear shook his head, clearly not agreeing with me. "Be that as it may, you don't owe these guys anything. It's not on you to nurse them back to health or give them your time so they can win you over."

"Maybe not, but I want to. At least for that first part. Walker got hurt because of me. I want to be here for him."

I think.

God, I was all twisted up inside.

"Take some time. Think about it. I'll be ready to leave the minute you say. You got me?"

Giving him a sharp nod, I leaned in and wrapped myself around him, needing one more hug.

"Gigi's gonna be pissed when she finds out how upset you are," he muttered. "You'd better do the talking. She won't want to hear it from me."

I nodded, knowing he was right. I'd been keeping her in the dark about a lot of things, but only because talking about them meant I had to examine my own feelings. "I'll call her in a bit."

Bear stiffened beside me, his head snapping to the side, his eyes narrowed. I followed his gaze, my body going tense when I saw the reason for his reaction.

Cross was walking back to the house. He looked miserable. I shouldn't care, but I did.

"Excuse me. I'm going to go have a little chat with your husband."

"Jonah, wait."

He froze in the middle of standing. I rarely used his real name, so he knew it was serious.

"Just don't kill him or anything," I eventually muttered, realizing there was nothing I could do or say to stop Bear from protecting me. I'd have better luck trying to stop a meteor from crashing into Earth.

"I'm only going to maim him a little."

"No. He's not the one I'm upset with. Not really."

"Coulda fooled me."

"He was just the messenger. A lot of the stuff he did, it was in the past and I've already forgiven him."

He pointed at my face, at the still-damp tear tracks on my cheeks. "That doesn't look like forgiveness."

"These tears aren't for him."

"He's still the one who made you cry. That means I get to bust his balls a little."

I let out a soft huff of laughter. "Fine. That's better than murder or maiming."

"Agree to disagree, cub. But we'll do it your way this once."

I jumped up and wrapped my arms around his barrel chest, squeezing hard. "What would I do without you?"

Bear pressed a kiss to the top of my head. "Good thing you'll never have to find out, huh?"

"Love you, Jonah," I said softly, letting him go. "Thank you for coming all the way down here. For listening to me and letting me snot all over your shirt for the last hour. For . . . for being the big brother I never asked for but desperately needed."

Bear blinked, his eyes suspiciously moist. He cleared his throat a few times before making some unintelligible noises, then managed a rough, "You too, kid."

I had to laugh at the big biker and his inability to handle his emotions. Some things were universal.

He punched me softly on the shoulder, like he'd done since we first met. "Why don't you go up to your room and rest a bit. Watch a movie or shower or something. I'll come check on you in a while."

That sounded like exactly what I needed. Quiet. No handsome cowboys to distract me from figuring out what I really wanted from my life.

"Good idea. Thanks again, Jonah. Really."

He gave me a slight grunt in response, then turned away and walked in the direction Cross had been going. I sent up a silent prayer busting balls wasn't going to be a literal expression.

I SLID DEEPER into the tub, the tips of my toes only just peeking out from the mountain of bubbles. If I could get away with it, I would live right here. I could conduct all my business via the phone, and whenever the bath got cold, I'd just refill it with the endless supply of hot water. Sure, I might turn into a prune, but there were worse things.

The music playing on my phone faded out and started again. It had been doing that pretty regularly since the moment I started the bath. Text messages. Every time one came through, my playlist was interrupted. I'd have to look at them soon.

When two more came through in rapid succession, I realized soon was now.

I sat up with a sigh and a slosh of water as I reached for my phone.

My heart lurched at the name on the first message.

CROSS:

I know you're angry. You have every right to be. I just wanted you to know that I'm doing my best to respect your wishes and give you space. Just . . . let me know you're okay? It's killing me not being able to hold you right now.

Not even two minutes later, he'd sent a follow-up.

CROSS:

I'm sorry.

My chest hurt. It took a lot for that man to apologize for anything, but the truth was, he didn't need to offer this one.

Unable to reply to him just yet, I clicked on the next text.

WALKER:

Guess who has two thumbs and just took himself to the bathroom?

WALKER:

Me. I'm the guy.

WALKER:

That sounded sexier in my head. I just thought you'd be interested in my solo hygiene victories. You know, in case that was the reason you hadn't come for a visit today.

WALKER:

You there, darlin'?

WALKER:

Damn, I wish there was a delete button.

He'd sent these in fairly rapid succession, and I could practically hear him overthinking everything since I hadn't responded.

"It's me. I'm the asshole, aren't I?" I said into the empty room before I set my phone down and sank all the way under the water.

I felt guilty for not immediately responding and easing his fears, but I didn't know how much Walker had known about my dad and his involvement in their family business. It felt like everyone had been keeping secrets from me my whole life, especially the ones I trusted most. Finding out he'd been part of the cover-up . . . I just didn't think I could take the betrayal right now. And until I knew, I couldn't pretend everything was normal between us.

I came up for air, gasping, heart pounding, but more focused than I had been a few minutes earlier.

My phone stared at me accusingly. I had to answer them eventually.

Next on my list of unanswered messages was Bishop. The last of which had come through not even fifteen minutes ago.

STERLING:

Missing you today, siren.

STERLING:

I know you're busy entertaining your friend, but think you might be able to slip away for a little while and come give me a kiss?

STERLING:

Or maybe I'll just come steal one when you least expect it.

Smiling, I snapped a photo of my bare legs, all the way to the tops of my thighs, in the water and sent it along with a response.

ME:

Now's your chance, secret agent man.

The text was marked as read, but there was no reply from the super spy, which left me with a sinking disappointment. Logically I knew I couldn't expect him to drop everything just to come kiss me, even if I hoped that's exactly what would happen.

Distracting myself, I washed my body with the fragrant soap Cross had supplied, then closed my eyes as I leaned my head on the sloped edge of the tub and just tried to clear my mind.

"Well, isn't this a pretty picture." Bishop's voice caressed my ear seconds later, sending me shrieking and flailing as I slid back into the water.

I came up spluttering in the least sexy way possible, meeting his amused gaze with a hard stare.

"You scared the shit out of me."

To his credit, Bishop tried to hide his smile. "Sorry, baby. I thought with that invitation you sent, you'd be expecting me."

"I would've if you'd answered me."

"Didn't I? I definitely answered you in my head."

My lips twitched because he looked just flustered enough for that to be true. "What did you say?"

"Pretty sure it was a prayer of some sort. Might have been unintelligible caveman-like grunts. You bring out the Neanderthal in me."

"That's a new line."

"Not a line when it's the truth, siren."

I tipped my chin up, offering my lips. "Well, you came here for a kiss. Aren't you going to steal one?"

"Is it stealing when you're offering it freely?"

"Sterling?"

"Yeah, baby?"

"Shut up and kiss me."

The hungry groan that escaped him came a second before he lowered to his knees and cupped the back of my head. His kiss was tender but edged with an almost untamed desire for more. It was over before I was ready for it to be, and a little whine escaped when he pulled away.

"I don't have time to climb in there with you and turn all these thoughts into reality, so we're both going to have to settle for a single kiss. For now."

Sighing, I pulled my knees to my chest and gazed at him. "Fine. Go do your stupid job."

He stared into my eyes, his face close enough I felt like he could see into my soul. "What's going on with you, siren?" I shook my head, but he grabbed my chin and forced me to look at him. "You're upset. What happened?"

For the briefest of moments, I thought maybe I'd brush him off. But something about Bishop made me unable to keep the truth from him.

"Cross told me some stuff earlier about my dad. What kind of man he really was."

"And?"

"It's bad. No one in my life is who I thought they were. Except for you."

He raised a brow. "As much as I appreciate being on your pedestal, we both know that's not true, siren. I have as many secrets as anyone else. Namely, my real reason for being here."

"But—"

"If I hadn't been outed right in front of you, you still wouldn't know the truth, baby. And that sucks, but it is what it is. People keep secrets for all sorts of reasons, most of them selfish, but a lot of them to protect the ones who matter most. Don't be so hard on your dad. He was as human as the rest of us. He's allowed to make mistakes."

"But they're bad, Bishop. They've done terrible things."

"So have I. So has your friend Bear. So have you, for that matter."

My skin crawled. "What do you mean by that?"

"If you think I didn't run a background check on him the moment I found out about you, you'd be dead wrong. He's involved in some dark shit, and so are you. Your dad was no different, just better at hiding it. Doesn't make his love for you less. Or yours for him. Just makes him a man."

My lower lip quivered. I don't know why I hadn't thought about it that way. Maybe I would have come to the realization in time, but it seemed so obvious when Bishop laid it out like that. I was more like my dad than I ever realized. It made me feel closer to him and soothed the sting of his betrayal.

"I guess you're right."

"For what it's worth, I'm sorry you had to learn the truth."

"I'm not," I said, realizing it was true. I'd rather know the truth and live with the fallout than stay in the dark.

He tipped my head back and began washing my hair in silence. I appreciated the touches he gave me, probably more than he knew. Still, I wanted more.

"You could always blow off your responsibilities and get in here with me," I teased, but my voice was breathy.

"I've thought about our first time more than once, baby. It doesn't involve a tub."

"Oh? What does it involve?"

"You, naked, at my mercy."

"What else?"

"Lots of fucking orgasms."

"Count me in. When do we start?"

He groaned. "You're definitely a siren."

"I mean, I'm already naked and wet."

This time he dunked me before standing. When I came up, he was adjusting himself, and his eyes were blazing as I laughed.

"Leave your door unlocked tonight."

I wasn't laughing anymore. "Okay."

With a final burning look, he left me as silently as he'd come. And I realized there was no way I could leave. Not him. Not Walker. And not Cross.

For better or worse, my future was tied to theirs.

twenty-five

. . .

River

The soft sound of my door opening pulled me from sleep. I hadn't meant to doze off, but the stress of the conversation I'd had with Cross had done a number on me, and after that hot bath, I couldn't keep my eyes open. Not even with the promise of Bishop visiting in the night.

I blinked a few times, trying to clear the sleep from my eyes, but with the lights out, I couldn't make out more than a shadowy figure standing between me and the still-open door. Soft light filtered in from the hallway, but it wasn't enough to do more than illuminate Bishop's bulky shape.

"So you did show up. I was worried if I fell asleep you'd just leave me to rest." I sat up and flashed him a smile he probably couldn't see. "Are you going to stand there staring, or are you going to shut the damn door and get over here?"

The figure froze, as if my voice startled him. Then he prowled closer without a word. Excitement zinged through me at the prospect of finally getting Bishop inside me. But there was something else there too. A little shiver of *not right* skittering down the back of my neck.

"Sterling . . . say something," I whispered. I hated how needy the request made me feel, but after the day I'd had, I just needed the reassurance of his voice. To know that he was here with me and even if I couldn't touch him the way I wanted to, that this was still special.

He held a finger up to his lips, the gesture so unlike my Sterling I stiffened. This wasn't Bishop. Curling my legs up, I prepared to launch myself off the other side of the bed so I could put space between myself and the approaching stranger.

"Who the fuck are you?" I hissed.

He didn't answer, but he was blocking my exit.

Instinct screamed at me to find another.

I didn't waste any time. There had been too many fucked up things happening lately for me to risk a single second. I threw my body toward the other side of the bed and the window just beyond it. My only thought was to get out of this room and as far away from this asshole as I could.

Rough fingers gripped my ankle, drawing a shriek from me as the stranger reeled me across my rumpled bedding and back toward him.

"No! Bishop! Cross! Walker, oh God, please."

He pinned my arms to my sides with hands like steel bands. Breath hot and reeking of cigarettes, his lips brushed my ear as he rasped with menacing calm, "No one is coming for you, malyshka."

My stomach roiled, and if I'd had anything to eat, I'm sure I would have lost all of it then and there.

This was so much worse than I thought. Volkov had gotten tired of waiting and sent one of his men after me. The only way this man was leaving without me was if he was the one in a body bag. I couldn't let him take me.

Leaning forward as far as I could, I brought my head back hard and fast, praying I'd connect with his nose. Pain burst across the back of my head as I did just that, and the satisfying crunch of his cartilage disintegrating sent a thrill through me. He just had to let go. Even if only slightly.

Instead he squeezed me tighter, his voice dripping with venom. "This could have been easy. My orders were only to bring you in alive. They didn't say anything about the condition you were in when I dropped you off."

"Cross!" I screamed, but he shut me up with a tight fitting gag across my lips.

"You're much prettier with something stuffed in your mouth." He jerked my hands behind my back and bound my wrists with the precision of someone who'd done it a time or twenty. "Time to go."

Then he tossed me over his shoulder, flailing and screaming through the gag. All I could hope was that one of my men would stop him.

Walker

A HEAVY THUMP from above had me squinting up at the ceiling.

"What the hell you doing up there, ladybug? Having a midnight dance party?" I glanced over at the clock on the bedside table of my temporary room on the first floor only to remember there wasn't one. It was weird not being surrounded by my usual stuff, but the convenience of not having to deal with stairs made it a lot more palatable.

I snagged my phone, ignoring the multiple texts I'd sent her with no answer. I didn't know what I'd done to piss her off, but as soon as I saw her, I'd sure as shit do my best to fix it.

ME:

You awake? Come down for a snuggle.

There was no read receipt, let alone a response, and no additional scuffles for me to gauge whether she'd even heard her phone go off. Maybe it was a stupid overreaction, but something about the situation wasn't sitting right.

I'd been sleeping in the room below hers for a few nights now and had never heard a peep from her.

Why tonight? What was she doing? Redecorating? Seemed like

something she'd do if she was stewing on a problem. Lord knows Cross had given her more than enough reason to blow off some steam.

A noise filtered through the quiet house. Maybe a shout? I couldn't quite tell what it was, but the hairs on the back of my neck stood on end.

Something was fucking wrong. Goddammit, something was wrong, and I couldn't do anything to help.

Knowing there was nothing I could do to personally check the situation out, I hit Cross's speed dial on my phone. He answered on the first ring.

"You okay?"

"Something's wrong. Check on River. I think I heard a shout."

He hung up without another word, and I knew he was on it.

But that uneasy feeling in my stomach only grew, so I searched for another number on my phone. This time the call was picked up on the second ring.

"Bishop."

"I think River's in trouble."

I heard the familiar sound of a clip being loaded before Bishop said, "I'll get her."

"Wait—" I started, but he'd already hung up. With a sigh, I looked down at my phone and finished what I'd been trying to say. "Someone should let Bear know."

I'd call him myself, but I didn't have his number. How could I have known I'd need to be a one-man phone tree?

I felt so fucking useless lying in my bed waiting for one or both of them to get back to me with news. My heart was racing, my breaths uneven. And then everything stopped as the distinctive crack of a gunshot rang out through the house.

Cross

RIVER HAD me all twisted up inside, and there wasn't a damn thing I could do about it. I'd promised myself I'd give her the night, let her have space to process everything I'd told her. But fuck me, it was harder than I'd thought. I wanted nothing more than to make her smile again, have her look at me like she had when she took me into her, and maybe, just maybe, hear her say she loved me again.

But all that had to wait, and I had to hope she'd come around.

I glanced down at the phone clutched in my hand. I checked it every few minutes just to torture myself with the knowledge that she still hadn't responded to any of my messages. While I was thumbing through our message thread, my phone vibrated with an incoming call.

Walker. Shit. Did he need his meds? Did he try to take himself to the bathroom again? Was I going to find him on the floor with his ass hanging out like last time?

I hit answer, my thoughts a tornado of increasingly more involved scenarios.

"You okay?"

"Something's wrong. Check on River. I think I heard a shout."

Before I could reply, River's faint scream of my name had me bolting out of bed, my phone clattering to the floor, forgotten.

"River!" I shouted, catching myself before I could burst through my bedroom door.

My gun. I needed to grab my gun.

Each second felt like a lifetime as I spun around and snatched it from my bedside drawer, doing a quick check to make sure it was loaded before I resumed my frantic race to get to her. A crash came from the stairs, sounds of a struggle following, and that was all I needed to flick the safety off and train my gun in front of me.

Heart pounding, I raced toward the noise, catching sight of her open bedroom door at the end of the hall. I couldn't quite make sense of the shadow at the top of the stairs in what little light the hallway offered, so I took a few more running steps and slapped my hand against the light switch, activating the custom antler chandelier. The entire main floor and the central part of this hallway lit up.

River was bound and gagged, thrown across the shoulder of a beast of a man. He was dressed head to toe in black, the balaclava he wore hid his fucking face, but that didn't matter. He was dead either way. I didn't need to know who he was to put him in the ground.

"Put my wife down, right the fuck now!" I screamed, cocking the gun and waiting for a clear shot.

Dead blue eyes met mine. "Are you so sure the whore is yours?"

Of course this was one of Volkov's goons. Part of me had known that would be the case the second I spotted the intruder. No one else would be so bold.

Or stupid.

River struggled against his hold, muffled shouting coming from behind the gag. Her legs flailed, and my girl landed a kick right to the fucker's groin. He let out a pained grunt, but stayed standing.

If not for her body draped across his, I'd risk a shot. But one wrong move, and I'd take her out with him. I couldn't take that risk. Instead I was forced to watch as the Russian bastard pulled out a gun of his own, brandishing it in front of him as he made his way down the stairs and toward my front door.

Panic tightened my chest. I couldn't let him get out the door with her. If he did, I'd never see her again.

"Stay down, sparrow." Taking the stairs as fast as I could, I closed in on him, firing one shot when she lay flat against his back.

The bullet went wide, shattering a longhorn skull mounted on the wall.

Fuck.

That was it. My only chance. This asshole wouldn't let me get another shot off.

Neither of us counted on the burly motherfucker storming out of his guest room like an enraged bull. Bear roared and sprinted for the would-be kidnapper. I could practically see the gears in his head turning. River's protector was planning on taking them both down with a brutal tackle. She'd get a little banged up, but she'd live. The Russian wouldn't be as lucky. I was willing to bet the biker had killed more than one man with his bare hands. Even as I was cheering him on, wishing I could do it myself, the Russian proved me for a fool.

In one seamless move, he twisted, and a gunshot rang out before any of us registered where it had been aimed.

Bear went down with a groan, blood dribbling out of the smoking wound right between his eyes. The floor and white tufted suede bench behind him were splattered with gore and stained crimson. River couldn't see her friend, and I sent up a silent prayer her captor wouldn't turn around.

My prayer wasn't answered. He turned, giving her a full view of the remains of the man she considered a brother. She screamed and thrashed so hard he almost dropped her. Hope bloomed inside me that this was the moment she'd get free, but he yanked her down until she was still in his hold but covering his entire chest before he pistol-whipped her so hard she went limp.

"One more step and she dies, Cross." The menacing words were spat with such fierce determination I didn't dare call his bluff.

"I will find you, motherfucker. And when I do, you'll wish you were dead."

The Russian laughed. "Good luck with that."

Hopeless fury burned through me as he backed out of the front door, his gun trained on River's temple the whole way. I had no recourse. Not a goddamn thing I could do. This asshole had not only broken into my house, he was getting away with my wife. And I was fucking letting him.

"Fuck!" I roared, my body shaking with the need to mete out punishment. I'd never been so scared and so damn useless in my entire life.

"Cross!" Walker bellowed, frustration and terror lacing his voice as he hobbled into the foyer, one hand holding onto the wall for dear life. He was clearly in pain. While he'd just been put in a walking cast for his broken leg, the burns on the bottom of his feet weren't quite healed enough to take him standing on them. His skin was pale and dotted with sweat, and he was swaying where he stood, but had our roles been reversed, I would have done the same thing. "What the fuck is happening?"

God, how was I going to tell him I lost her?

I had to. He had to know because I was going to need all hands on deck to get her back.

Before I managed to come up with something, Bishop barreled down the hallway, heading toward us from the back of the house.

"Where is she?" he demanded, eyes sharp, but there was no masking the worry in his tone.

"Where the fuck have you been?" I snapped. "They took her right out from under us. Walked her out the damn door."

"You just let them take her?" Walker rasped.

"Who, Cross? Who took her?" The fear in Bishop's voice echoed my own.

"The Russians have her. He killed Bear, had a gun to her head. I couldn't . . . Jesus, I couldn't stop him."

Whatever force had kept Walker upright left him. He sagged to the floor with a strangled whimper. "We have to get her back. We have to find her. We have to. They'll hurt her."

"Don't worry. Volkov is using her as leverage. He won't do anything that threatens his ability to blackmail us."

"You think he's going to ask for a ransom?" Walker asked.

I started to nod, but Bishop stopped me dead. His voice was hollow and defeated. "If we're lucky, that's what he'll do. But his fight with you is deeper than money. You cut off his income stream and then sent his uncle to prison. Which makes this personal. He wants to hurt you as much as you hurt him."

How the fuck could my ranch hand know all this? Who was this guy? What did I actually know about Sterling Bishop?

"You shouldn't know that. Who the fuck are you?"

When his stormy eyes met mine, it was clear he knew what I was really asking. He didn't play dumb, didn't try and act like he hadn't been found out.

"Who I am doesn't matter. All you need to know is I'm the man who's going to bring your wife home. Alive."

more by meg & kim

Twisted Cross Ranch

A dark contemporary cowboy reverse harem

Sinner's Secret

Corruptor's Claim

Deadly Debt

the mate games universe

By K. Loraine & Meg Anne

War

Obsession

Rejection

Possession

Temptation

Pestilence

Promised to the Night (Prequel Novella)

Deal with the Demon

Claimed by the Shifters

Captive of the Night

Lost to the Moon

Death

Haunting Beauty

Hunted Beast

Hateful Prince

Heartless Villain

also by meg anne

Brotherhood of the Guardians/Novasgard Vikings

Undercover Magic *(Nord & Lina)*

A Sexy & Suspenseful Fated Mates PNR

Hint of Danger

Face of Danger

World of Danger

Promise of Danger

Call of Danger

Bound by Danger (Quinn & Finley)

The Chosen Universe

The Chosen

A Fated Mates High Fantasy Romance

Mother Of Shadows

Reign Of Ash

Crown Of Embers

Queen Of Light

The Chosen Boxset #1

The Chosen Boxset #2

The Keepers

A Guardian/Ward High Fantasy Romance

The Dreamer (A Keeper's Prequel)

The Keepers Legacy

The Keepers Retribution

The Keepers Vow

The Keepers Boxset

<u>The Forsaken</u>

A Rejected Mates/Enemies-To-Lovers Romantasy

Prisoner of Steel & Shadow

Queen of Whispers & Mist

Court of Death & Dreams

Prince of Sea & Stars

A Standalone MMF Romantasy Adventure

<u>Gypsy's Curse</u>

A Psychic/Detective Star-Crossed Lovers UF Romance

Visions Of Death

Visions Of Vengeance

Visions Of Triumph

The Gypsy's Curse: The Complete Collection

also by k. loraine

The Blackthorne Vampires

THE BLOOD TRILOGY

(Cashel & Olivia)

Blood Captive

Blood Traitor

Blood Heir

BLACKTHORNE BLOODLINES

(Lucas & Briar)

Midnight Prince

Midnight Hunger

THE WATCHER SERIES

Waking the Watcher

Denying the Watcher

Releasing the Watcher

THE SIREN COVEN

Eternal Desire (Shifter reluctant mates)

Cursed Heart (Hate to Lovers)

Broken Sword (MMF menage Arthurian)

STANDALONES

Cursed (MFM Sleeping Beauty Retelling)

REVERSE HAREM STANDALONES

Their Vampire Princess (A Reverse Harem Romance)

All the Queen's Men (A Fae Reverse Harem Romance)

about meg anne

USA Today and international bestselling paranormal and fantasy romance author Meg Anne has always had stories running on a loop in her head. They started off as daydreams about how the evil queen (aka Mom) had her slaving away doing chores, and more recently shifted into creating backgrounds about the people stuck beside her during rush hour. The stories have always been there; they were just waiting for her to tell them.

Like any true SoCal native, Meg enjoys staying inside curled up with a good book and her fur babies . . . or maybe that's just her. You can convince Meg to buy just about anything if it's covered in glitter or rhinestones, or make her laugh by sharing your favorite bad joke. She also accepts bribes in the form of baked goods and Mexican food.

Meg is best known for her leading men #MenbyMeg, her inevitable cliffhangers, and making her readers laugh out loud, all of which started with the bestselling Chosen series.

about k. loraine

USA Today Bestselling author Kim Loraine writes steamy contemporary and sexy paranormal romance. **You'll find her paranormal romances written under the name K. Loraine and her contemporaries as Kim Loraine.** Don't worry, you'll get the same level of swoon-worthy heroes, sassy heroines, and an eventual HEA.

When not writing, she's busy herding cats (raising kids), trying to keep her house sort of clean, and dreaming up ways for fictional couples to meet.

www.ingramcontent.com/pod-product-compliance
Lightning Source LLC
Chambersburg PA
CBHW020501310726
48979CB00016B/2752/J

* 9 7 8 1 9 6 1 7 4 2 0 7 9 *